Polly's Senior Year At Boarding School

Dorothy Whitehill

Polly's Senior Year At Boarding School

CHAPTER I

SENIORS!

Polly Pendleton and Lois Farwell returned to Seddon Hall as seniors.

Up the long hill that led from the station their carriage crawled as it had done on every other opening day.

From the summit of the hill the low, red-roofed buildings of the school smiled a welcome from their setting of blazing Autumn leaves, and all around them girls were calling out greetings.

There was a marked change in the two girls' outward appearances – their hair was up and their skirts were longer, their whole bearing was older. They were different from the two youngsters whose Freshman year has already been recorded. That is, they looked different, and if you had asked them about it they would have assured you that they were indeed different.

But, the old-time twinkle in Polly's eyes and Lois' sudden merry laugh gave you a comforting feeling that, after all, in spite of assurances and looks, they were still the same Polly and Lois.

Nothing very eventful had happened in either one of their lives, during the past years. They had spent their Winters at Seddon Hall and their vacations at Polly's old home in New England with Mrs. Farwell. Polly's uncle, Mr. Pendleton, and Dr. Farwell, had come up on visits when they could. Bob, Lois' big brother, had come, too, but less frequently of late. He was at college now and working very hard.

They had made new friends, but, what is more important, they had kept their old ones.

This well ordered way of living, however, had to change. Time had gone on slowly, but steadily and now, suddenly, they were Seniors. It was an exhilarating thought and Polly and Lois hugged each other whenever it struck them afresh.

Their carriage finally reached the door. In a second they were in the reception room, and, after they had greeted Mrs. Baird and the faculty, they dashed up the front stairs—a privilege only accorded the Seniors—and found their room, a big corner one, which they were to share in Senior Alley. Rooming together was another Senior privilege.

"Poll, we're back." Lois threw her suitcase without regard to contents on one of the beds and looked around her.

"Yes, we're back, and we're Seniors and, what's more, we've the best room on the Alley," Polly answered, enthusiastically. "We'll put your window box there." She indicated a broad bow window, overlooking the campus and gym. "And we'll—"

"Oh! don't let's fuss about the decorations now," Lois interrupted. "Let's find Betty and the other girls. I'm dying to know who's back."

"I am too, sort of," Polly agreed reluctantly, as they left the room and started for the Assembly Hall. "Do you know, Lo, I always feel funny about the new girls."

"Why?"

"Oh, I can't exactly explain, but I don't like them; I wish they hadn't come. We were so all right last year. Why couldn't just the old girls come back and go on where we left off?"

"Why, you silly," Lois laughed. "Some of last year's girls were new and you liked them. Anyway, cheer up, and don't worry about it now. Listen to the racket they're making in the hall."

Polly gave herself a little shake, a trick she had when she wanted to dismiss a thought from her mind, but her face failed to reflect Lois' smile of anticipation. She was a queer puzzle, was Polly. Uncle Roddy once described her as a tangle of deep thoughts, completely surrounded by a sense of humor. And Mrs. Farwell always insisted that she discussed the weightiest problems of life when she was running for a trolley. Lois was the exact opposite, an artist, a dreamer of dreams, who, when her mind was off on some airy flight, was maddeningly indifferent to everything

3

else. They were ideal friends, for they acted as a balance, the one for the other. They were so much together that no one ever thought of them singly.

A shout of welcome from the old girls, and eager silence from the new ones, greeted their entrance into the Assembly Hall. There was a hubbub of hellos for a minute, and then Betty descended upon them.

Betty, the freckled face—she wasn't a bit changed. She still wore a ribbon on her hair, and her nose was as snubbed and impudent as ever. Of course, she was taller and her skirts were longer, but no one realized it. That was the difference. With Polly and Lois the years had really added themselves and marked a change, but Betty was still Betty and years mattered not at all.

"Jemima!" she exclaimed, joyfully, "but I'm glad you've come. What under the sun did you wait until the late train for. I've been here all day and I've felt like a fish out of water. There's a raft of new girls, but no Senior specials, thank goodness. The two Dorothys are here,"—she paused and wrinkled her nose just the least little bit in disapproval, and then rushed on. "I'm rooming with Angela, you know. Isn't it mean Connie isn't back? Ange misses her already."

Constance Wentworth, of whom she spoke, was one of the old girls and Angela Hollywood's chosen companion. She had not returned this year because her music professor had insisted upon her starting in at the Conservatory of Music, for she was a remarkable pianist. The girls realized that no one would ever quite fill her place.

"Where is Ange?" Lois inquired, when Betty paused for breath.

"In her room, I mean our room; she's moping," Betty answered. "She said three distinct times that she wished Connie were back, and so I left. I'm not sensitive, but—" Betty left the rest unsaid, but her look expressed volumes.

"Poor Ange!" Polly said with exaggerated feeling. "I don't blame her; let's go find her; she must need cheering up; besides, I'm tired of meeting new girls."

Angela answered their knock a few minutes later with a "Come in," uttered in her own particular drawl. She was sitting on her bed in the midst of clothes. Apparently, she had made little or no progress in unpacking her suitcase, for nothing was put away.

Angela had always been, and was still, the unrivaled beauty of Seddon Hall. Her complexion was as soft and pink as a rose petal, and her shimmering golden hair and big blue eyes made you think of gardens and Dresden china. She was never known to hurry, and she spoke with a soft lazy drawl, which, curiously enough, never irritated any one. She had won quite a renown as a poet, but was too quiet to be generally popular.

"Hello, you three!" she greeted, as the girls entered. "I'm awfully glad you're back. Isn't this a mess?" She included the room with a wave of her arm. "I don't know where to begin."

"It's exactly the way it was when I left you," Betty exclaimed with pretended wrath.

"I know it; but you've been so piggy with the dresser drawers and the wardrobe that there's no room for my things," Angela teased back.

She was apparently willing to leave the argument so, for as the girls dropped into comfortable positions on the floor and window seat, she discarded the shoe she was holding, stuffed a pillow behind her and folded her hands. Her guests stayed until dinner time and talked. It was almost a class meeting; for it was a well established fact that when these four girls decided anything the rest of the class agreed with an alacrity that was very flattering to their good judgment.

It was not until Mrs. Baird, who sat at the Senior table the first night as a special favor, asked them if they had discovered any homesick new girls, that they realized that as Seniors, holding responsible positions in the school, they had failed already.

After dinner they stopped to consult on the Bridge of Sighs—the covered way that connected the two main buildings of the school.

"Well, what's to be done?" inquired Lois. "Instead of deciding what color shoes we'd wear at commencement we should have been drying somebody's eyes."

"Quite right," Betty mimicked Lois' righteous tones. "We were very selfish; in fact, I'm ashamed of us. Let's go to Assembly Hall and be giddy little cheerers up."

Polly laughed.

"Oh, Bet, be sensible! Hasn't your observation in the past taught you that homesick girls don't go to Assembly Hall to cry? They tuck their silly heads under their protecting pillows in their own room. Let's go to Freshman Lane."

"Why Freshman?" Angela inquired softly. "Freshmen are too young and excited to be homesick so soon. Let's go to the Sophs quarters."

They went, tapping gently at every door all the way down the corridor, but received no response.

"They're a heartless lot," Betty declared at the last door. "Not one of them in tears. It's not right, they're entirely too cheerful for so young a class." And she scowled wrathfully as an indication of her displeasure.

"Never mind, Bet," Lois laughed, "maybe we'll have better luck with the Juniors."

Betty took heart and led the way.

Lois was right, though the doleful sobs that met their ears at the door of Junior Mansions — nicknamed the year before because the present Seniors had been so very elegant — could hardly be called luck.

"Jemima!" Betty exclaimed. "A deluge, our search proves fruitful at last."

Polly went to the door through which the sounds came and pushed it open.

The room was dark. The light from the hall cast a streak over the bare floor and discovered a heap of something half on, and half off the bed. At one side of the room a wicker suitcase stood beside the dresser, its swelling sides proclaimed it still unpacked. A hat and coat were flung on the chair — but these were minor details. The heart-breaking sobs filled every corner of the room, and the figure on the bed heaved convulsively with each one.

Polly was the first to speak.

"What's the matter, homesick?" she asked cheerfully as she pressed the electric button and flooded the room with light.

On closer inspection they saw that the girl had heaps of black hair that had become unfastened and lay in a heavy coil on the bed. Also, she had on a crumpled silk waist and a dark green skirt.

Lois and Betty helped her on to the bed and Polly bathed her face with cold water. Angela was tongue-tied, but she patted her hand and murmured incoherent things. Finally the sobs stopped.

"We've got to get her out of here," Lois whispered. "Don't you want to do up your hair and come down to the Assembly Hall?" she said aloud. "Everybody's dancing."

The new girl — she was still just the new girl, for she had refused to tell her name, or say one word — sat up and smoothed her waist.

Betty sighed with relief.

"Come on, that's right," she said encouragingly. "Don't mind about your eyes, all the other new girls will have red ones too. Why when I was a new girl," she said grandly, "I cried for weeks."

Polly and Lois and Angela gasped. Betty had never been known to shed a tear. As for weeks of them, that was a bit extravagant. But the fib had the desired effect. The new girl turned her large, drenched gray eyes on Betty and studied her carefully.

"I reckon you looked something like a picked buzzard when you got through," she said with a broad Southern accent.

There was an astonished silence for a second, then the girls burst into peals of laughter. It was contagious, happy laughter, and the new girl, after a hesitating minute, joined in. After that, it was an easy matter to make conversation and to persuade her to leave her room.

The girls found out that she was Fanny Gerard, and had come straight from South Carolina. Her father — she had no mother — had brought her to school and then returned to the city by the next train. Unfortunately, it had been Miss Hale, the Latin teacher — nicknamed the Spartan years before by

7

Betty, the only unpopular teacher in Seddon Hall—who had shown Fanny to her room.

"She just opened the do' and pointed at that little old plain room with her bony finger and said: 'This is you alls room, Miss Gerard,' and left me. I tell you I like to died."

The tears threatened to burst forth again. Betty and Polly hastened to explain that the Spartan was not even to be considered as part of Seddon Hall. And they brought back the smiles when they explained that the Bridge of Sighs was so named because the Spartan's room was at the end of it.

All together, they made a very satisfactory cure and when they left Fanny for the night, after having unpacked her suitcase for her, she was quite bright and contented.

"What do you think of her?" Polly demanded, when she and Lois were alone, after the good night bell.

Lois considered a minute.

"She's rare, and I think she's going to be worth cultivating. Certainly she's funny," she said.

"Seddon Hallish, you mean?" Polly inquired.

"No, not exactly."

"She couldn't take Connie's place for instance?"

"Never in a thousand years!"

"Lois."

"Yes."

"You're thinking about the same thing I am."

"What are you thinking of?"

"The five boy's pictures she brought in her suitcase."

"Yes, I was. Sort of silly of her. Maybe they are her brothers."

"They're not, she's an only child."

"Well, all Southern girls are sentimental." Polly was almost asleep.

"Maybe we can cure her," she said.

"Maybe," Lois answered drowsily.

"We're Seniors, Lo."

"Yes. This is the first night of our last year."

"I know, pretty much all right rooming together, isn't it?"

"You bet."

"Goodnight."

"Goodnight."

CHAPTER II

A CLASS MEETING

"Really Lo, I think its downright inconsiderate of you to be for Princeton." Polly was standing on a chair which threatened every minute to topple from its precarious position on her bed and she was struggling with a huge Harvard banner. She made the above statement with spirit.

Lois, on the other side of the room, was in nearly the same position, only she was struggling with a Princeton banner.

"I don't see why," she answered Polly's remark casually, and went on tacking.

"Because that awful orange color simply fights with my crimson. We can't have them in the same room."

Lois descended to the floor and surveyed the two banners.

"No, we can't," she said decidedly. "Mine goes better with the room than yours, don't you think?" she asked, after a pause, with just a little too much show at indifference.

"No, I don't." Polly's reply was prompt. "Color scheme doesn't matter to me anyway, but Bob's flag is going up somewhere."

Fortunately, at this moment Betty burst into the room.

"News, good news," she exclaimed. "The Art teacher has just arrived and I've met her. She's a duck. Hello, what's the matter?" she inquired, suddenly interrupting herself. "Is this flag day, and do you really mean you are going to hang both those banners?"

"No, we're not," Lois answered, and Polly laughed.

"The trouble is, Bet, we can't decide which one we will hang. Lo, of course, with her artistic ideas, thinks the orange would go better with the browns of the rug and screen, and I want my Harvard banner up through sentiment. Bob gave it to me and he'll probably make the track this year and anyway, he's Lois' brother and she's always been for Harvard until

Frank decided on Princeton and gave her that." Polly gazed with resentment on the banner and Lois both.

"Did Frank give Lo that? Jemima! I didn't know they were such good friends."

Frank Preston was a cousin of Louise Preston, an old Seddon Hall girl Lois and Polly had met him three summers before, while they were visiting Louise, and Lois and he had kept up the friendship ever since.

"Of course he gave it to me, and Polly you know he had a thousand and one good reasons for going to Princeton. Harvard is not the only college."

"Only one I'd go to if I were a boy," Polly answered airily. "But what will we do? I can't hold this up all day."

Betty had a sudden inspiration.

"I'll tell you," she announced. "Take turns, Poll, you put yours up this week and Lo can have hers next, and there you are." She looked proud at having solved the difficulty.

"Bet, you're a genius!" Polly exclaimed, and Lois added her quota of praise.

"Put yours up first, Poll," she said.

But Polly protested.

"No, yours is up already; leave it, and mine can go up next week." So it was decided.

"Now, stop work and let's talk," Betty suggested. "Haven't you anything to eat?"

"Jam, crackers and peanut butter in the window box," Lois told her. "Get them out and tell us about the Art teacher; I'm going to go on hanging pictures."

"Well, she's a duck, I told you that, and an old friend of Mrs. Baird; her first name is Janet. I was standing in the hall when she arrived and I carried her bag to her room. She has the one next to the Spartan's, poor soul!"

"Well how do you know she's nice?" Polly insisted.

"Because she's something like Mrs. Baird."

"Oh, well, of course that's enough; she couldn't be just as nice."

"No, naturally not. There's only one Mrs. Baird, which reminds me — there's a young child" — Betty said the words with emphasis — "A Freshman, I think, who needs serious attention. I heard her fussing to-day; something was wrong and she said 'Mrs. Baird made her sick.'"

Lois looked horrified, but Polly only shrugged her shoulders.

"She won't last long," she said indifferently, and Betty felt ashamed of having bothered to give the child a lecture.

"When do we have a Class meeting?" she asked, to change the subject. "We've got to do something about the welcome dance."

"Why not now?" Lois stopped hammering. "Let's get the Seniors all in here."

It was only a matter of a few minutes before this was accomplished, for Betty went to rout them out.

Angela came first to be followed by the two Dorothys, then Mildred Weeks and Evelin Hatfield, two girls who had come to Seddon Hall the year before. Betty followed them.

"Everybody here?" she asked. "Don't you think we'd better elect officers first off? Then some one will be able to start things. Here's some paper," she added, tearing off sheets and passing them around.

But things were not to run so smoothly. One of the Dorothys rose to protest.

"Don't you think it would be more formal if we held a real meeting in one of the classrooms with Mrs. Baird there," she said. "Then we could have a ballot box and do the thing properly."

Polly and Lois exchanged glances. The Dorothys had always been dissenting voices ever since Freshman days.

Betty tore her hair in secret behind the wardrobe.

It was Angela's slow drawl that settled the question.

"It would be more formal," she agreed, "but what would be the use? Mrs. Baird is much too busy to come, the classrooms are always stuffy after school and besides, we couldn't take the jam along, it's against the rules."

Mildred and Evelin, who had been rather inclined to favor the Dorothys, were won over by this and the point was carried.

The meeting stayed where it was and the vote was cast. Lois was elected President; Angela, Treasurer; Betty, Editor of the school paper; and Polly, Secretary. When the congratulations were over they started with their plans for the welcome dance.

"Do let's have it different," beseeched Betty. "Last year it was awful. All the new girls cried and there wasn't enough ice cream."

"How can we make it different? There's nothing to do but dance." Dot Mead protested. She was not altogether happy over the election.

"Let's make more of a feature of the new girls," Mildred said shyly. "Last year I know Evelin and I felt awfully out of it. Couldn't we—"

"You've hit the nail on the head," Polly exclaimed. "We'll find some new idea of doing things so that the new girls will really feel it's their dance. Everybody think."

While these preparations were going on in the Senior Alley—another meeting, less important in character, but equally heated as to discussion, was raging in Freshman Lane.

Jane Ramsey, who had been at Seddon Hall for three years in the lower school and had at last reached the dignity of Freshman, was giving an admiring group of new girls some advice.

There were five of them, Catherine and Helen Clay, two sisters—Catherine a Freshman and Helen a Sophomore, Winifred Hayes, another Sophomore, and Phylis Guile. Phylis Guile could hardly be classed with the rest of the new girls. Her big sister Florence, who had been a Senior three years before, had told her all about Seddon Hall, and the thought of going anywhere else had never entered her head. She knew so much about everything, that Jane, whose ideas of being a Freshman meant having a chum, took to her at once, and they vowed eternal friendship.

Jane, whose hair was black, almost as black as her eyes, contrasted strangely with Phylis' dazzling fairness. At present, they were doing most of the talking.

"Do the new girls vote for Captain too?" Phylis asked. "Florence has told me of course, but I've forgotten."

"Yes, all the upper school," Jane told her.

They were talking of the coming basket ball election.

"But how do we know who to vote for?" demanded Helen. "We've never seen them play."

"You ask an old girl," Jane replied loftily. "As it happens, this year they'll all tell you the same thing."

"What?"

"Oh, I know," Phylis answered eagerly. "They'll tell you to vote for Polly Pendleton. Florence told me she played a wonderful game, and to be sure and vote for her."

"She does, too," Jane agreed with enthusiasm, "but so does Lois Farwell. I can't make up my mind which to choose, and it's awfully important."

"Is Polly the one that sits next to Mrs. Baird on the right," Catherine asked, "with the brown hair?"

"Yes, that's Polly."

"Well, I love her; she's so pretty; and, anyway, I'm going to vote for her," she finished.

"Who's the beautiful Senior with golden hair?" Winifred inquired. "I'd like to vote for her."

Jane laughed heartily. Sometimes news of the upper school leaked into the lower, and she had heard Angela's views on all strenuous sports.

"That's Angela Hollywood; she's awfully funny, but, oh dear, she can't play basket ball; why she's never even made the team."

"Tell us who'll make it this year?" Helen asked. "Do new girls ever get on?" she added wistfully.

"Polly was the only one who made it; that is for five years," Phylis explained; "she was a new girl and a Freshman. My sister's best friend, Louise Preston, was captain that year. I wish it would happen again; but no fear, I guess we'll have to wait."

"If we sit here talking about it, I'll begin to hope," and Jane jumped up and began brushing her hair. "It's time to dress anyway."

Her guests took the hint and departed, all except Phylis.

"That spoils it all," she said, when the door closed.

"All what?" Jane inquired.

"Why, I'd picked some flowers, and I was going to give them to Polly, but now if she's going to be the captain — it looks — "

"Nonsense; it does not," Jane contradicted. "Send them but don't be silly about it, Polly wouldn't think of letting you have a crush on her."

"Will you put your name on the card, too?" Phylis asked.

Jane considered. "I will if you send them to Lois, too," she said, thereby giving away a secret she had hoped to keep.

After the Senior meeting Polly decided she needed air.

"I'm going now, this minute," she declared. "I'm suffocated."

Lois, who had thrown herself down on the bed between laughter and tears, murmured a vague promise to follow. She changed her mind later and decided on a cold shower instead.

As she went down the stairs to Roman Alley, she heard some one stumble, and then the thud, thud, of falling boxes.

15

"Who is it, did you hurt yourself?" she called, and hurried around the turn of the stairs. A remarkably pretty woman looked up from a waterfall of canvases.

"No; but I deserved to, for carrying a lazy man's load," she laughed.

"Let me help," Lois offered, starting to pick up the canvases, "you must be Miss Crosby. Oh, but that's nice," she added suddenly, holding out a sketch at arm's length.

Miss Crosby smiled.

"Do you like it? I did it this summer. Are you interested in drawing?" she asked.

"Oh, yes!" Lois's tone was surprised — as if any one could doubt such a well known fact.

"Then you must be Lois Farwell," she said.

"Why, I am."

Miss Crosby's smile broadened. "I thought you were; you see Mrs. Baird told me — " she hesitated, "well it doesn't matter what. If you'll help me up with these things I'll be ever so grateful."

Together they carried all the pictures up to Miss Crosby's room, and Lois stood them up against the bed and walls, and then admired them.

Miss Crosby made her talk, and understood what she said, which was difficult for most people when Lois talked art. In fact she completely forgot she was Senior President, and had barely time to scramble into her dress and reach the platform to announce to the assembled old girls the plans for the coming dance.

It was not until after study hour that Polly and she returned to their room and found the flowers. Polly almost stepped on them as she opened the door.

"What under the sun?" Lois turned on the light. "Flowers? do look! To Polly and Lois from Jane and Phylis."

"Crushes," gasped Lois, "how awful!"

CHAPTER III

FANNY

Sundays, that is to say, Boarding School Sundays, are apt to be longer than any of the other days in the week.

Certainly it was so of Seddon Hall. Mrs. Baird thought the girls needed "time off to think," as she expressed it, so that, after the morning service in the little village church, the rest of the day was free.

It had always proved a good idea, for after a week spent in obedience to bells, a whole day to do as you please in, has an exhilarating effect.

But this particular first Sunday looked as if it were going to disprove the efficiency of the plan.

It was the day after the Welcome Dance to the new girls, and it was raining. Not a nice, heavy pouring rain, but a dreary persistent drizzle. The girls wandered aimlessly about the corridors in the most woe-begone fashion, for there was no chance of getting out of doors for a walk.

The dance the night before had proved a great success. Instead of each old girl taking a new girl, as had formerly been the custom, Polly's versatile brain had decided on a far better plan.

The new girls arrived in a body in Assembly Hall and were received by their class and formally introduced to one another. Then a daisy chain started and was so arranged that before it was over, every one had met and spoken to every one else in the school. By the time the refreshments arrived, all the girls were in a gale and not a tear was shed.

Sunday, however, was a different matter. Everybody felt damp and cold in church, and the sermon had been very long. Even Betty was out of sorts.

"Do you know," she said, crossly — she and Angela were in Polly's and Lois' room the early part of the afternoon. "I'm tired of us. We are all so afraid of letting anybody else into our select company that we are growing positively stuck up. Deny it, if you can," she persisted, as Polly looked up in surprise. "Here we sit like graven images, when we ought to be in Assembly Hall. Come on."

17

"Oh, Bet, you're so energetic," Angela drawled, "and we're so comfy."

"Assembly Hall won't be any fun," Polly protested. "I'm crazy to do something too, but—"

"Let's go get Fanny," Lois suggested. "She's bound to make us laugh. I was talking to her before church this morning. She was fussing about having to carry so many subjects; when she got to geometry she waxed eloquent. 'I declare there's no use my wasting my time on arithmetic,' she said, and when I told her there was a slight difference between the two, she wouldn't have it. 'It's all the same thing; maybe one's a tiny bit more elaborate than the other, but what's the use of proving all those angles equal. I don't reckon I'll ever be a carpenter; so there's just no sense in it.' I had to laugh at her," Lois finished.

"Oh, Fanny's rare," Betty agreed. "Let's go see if she's in her room instead of asking her down here. I'm tired of Senior Alley."

Polly and Lois agreed with alacrity, but Angela insisted she had letters to write and they left her knowing quite well there would be no jam left when they returned.

Fanny was in her room, but instead of opening the door to Polly's knock, she called out:

"Who all's there?"

"We are," Lois answered for them. "May we come in?"

The annoyed tone vanished from Fanny's voice.

"Oh, you all," she called; "come in, of course;"—and as they entered—"I thought maybe it was some of those impertinent young Freshmen coming to give me advice, and I just couldn't be bothered with them. That's why I didn't sound too cordial."

She was sitting on the floor in the middle of her room, surrounded by letters and bands of every color ribbon.

"I hope we're not disturbing you?" Polly said, rather taken aback at the sight of her. She couldn't quite understand all the letters, but she had her suspicions.

Betty found a place to sit, or rather perch, on the bed.

"Playing postoffice?" she asked with a grin.

But Fanny refused to be teased. She continued to sort out her letters, while she explained their presence.

"You see," she began dreamily, "these here notes are all from my boy friends; some of them are three years old."

"The friends?" queried Lois.

"No, stupid, the letters," Betty said hastily in an aside. "Yes, go on," she encouraged Fanny.

"And every now and then I like to read them over; some of them are awfully sweet, especially Jack's."

"Who's Jack?" her listeners demanded in chorus.

"Oh, Jack's my favorite admirer," she admitted, rather than stated. "He's crazy about me, or so he says. I reckon I'll just have to marry him one of these days. He's so handsome—" She paused, a sentimental smile of remembrance wreathing her face.

"How thrilling! do tell us," Betty begged. She was gurgling with joy inside, and like Polly and Lois, she was highly amused. They were all laughing at Fanny, rather than with her, which was unkind and inexcusable, as they had encouraged the recital, but her sentimental attitude was beyond their understanding.

Boys figured largely in all their thoughts, it's true, but in a totally different way. Polly, for instance, quite frankly admired Bob Farwell. She endowed him with every virtue. He was tremendously clever. He was the most wonderful athlete, and he loved dogs—especially Polly's dogs—in fact he was altogether perfect in her eyes—but she couldn't imagine tying up his letters in baby blue ribbons and keeping them in her top drawer.

And Lois, who was quite extravagantly fond of Frank Preston, would have repudiated and emphatically denied any suggestion of his being a suitor.

As for Betty—the idea of liking a boy just because he was handsome, was too foolish to even consider. The fact that Dick Saxon—supposedly her arch enemy, but really her best friend—had flaming red hair and was undeniably homely—may, of course, had something to do with her disgust for good looks. Like lots of other girls, The Three judged boys by their ability to do; while the road to Fanny's heart was by way of graceful and charming compliments.

"You were saying—" Polly interrupted Fanny's dream.

"Why, let me see—about Jack? He's really stunning in his uniform—he goes to military school—I have a lot of buttons off his coat."

At this point, Lois, much to the disgust of Polly and Betty, instead of waiting for more of Jack, inquired:

"Why have you all these colored ribbons to tie up your letters? I thought all love letters had to be tied in blue?"

Fanny picked up the various bands, looked at them while she went over in her mind whether or not she would tell them her special system. It was a clever idea, so she decided she would.

"Blue is for love letters," she told Lois, "because blue is true. I tie all Jack's letters in blue. Yellow means fickle—" She paused. "Well, there is a boy," she proceeded reluctantly, "down home, who used to like me until he met a cousin of mine, and she just naturally cut me out; so I tie his letters with yellow ribbon. This here green," she took up two letters tied with a narrow piece of baby ribbon, "is for hope."

"Hope?" Lois stifled a laugh. "Do you mean you hope for more?"

Fanny had heard the giggle and looked up in surprise. A little hurt look stole across her face.

"I reckon you all think I'm silly," she said, slowly, "but you see, down home, there's not much to do between holidays, when the boys come, except write letters and wait for mail, and all the girls I—"

She stopped; a big lump rose in her throat, and her eyes filled with tears.

The Three felt properly ashamed of themselves. Polly finally broke the embarrassed silence.

"We don't think you're silly at all," she fibbed consolingly. "If you want to keep your letters, why shouldn't you tie them up in appropriate colored ribbons?"

"But you wouldn't keep yours," Fanny replied with more insight than they had given her credit for.

"Well, no; I wouldn't, that is, I don't," Polly answered, lamely. And Betty seized the first opportunity to change the subject.

"What did you say about the Freshmen bothering?" she asked, when Fanny was in smiles again.

"They most certainly did, two of them, Jane and Phylis. They came in and wanted to know if I was homesick." Fanny looked indignant. "I told them no. Then they looked at all the pictures on my bureau, and Jane, the sassy little thing, told me if I wanted to get along at Seddon Hall, I'd have to stop being boy crazy. I just told them to go on about their business, right quick, and they went," she finished triumphantly.

"Jemima! the little—" Betty stopped from sheer astonishment. Polly and Lois exchanged understanding glances.

The next day all the girls assembled in the gym, a round building about a hundred feet from the school. A basket ball court took up most of the floor space. A balcony for spectators ran around three sides of the room. Every possible device hung from the ceiling, rings, ladders, trapezes and horizontal bars, but for the most part, these were dusty and disused.

Seddon Hall centered all its faculty on basket ball. Twice a year, in February and June, the team played outside schools and almost always came out victorious.

To-day, because it was raining still, most of the girls entered for the first try out. The Seniors sat in the balcony and watched, while every girl had a chance to pass the basket ball and try for a basket.

"Not a very likely crowd," Polly mused, "hardly a decent play."

21

"It's too early to tell, in all this mob," Lois answered.

"I'm dizzy watching them. I see that little imp of a Jane with Phylis Guile over in the corner. Let's go and thank them for the flowers?" she suggested.

Polly groaned — "All right, come on; you know we've got to put our foot — I mean feet down now hard, and I suppose we should talk to them about being so rude to Fanny. What do you suppose they really said?"

Jane and Phylis were sitting in front of the lockers. They saw the two Seniors coming towards them, but, because they were very much embarrassed, they pretended they didn't.

Lois started the conversation, rather abruptly. She was afraid to let Polly say much. Polly was a little bit too frank in her opinion, and Lois dreaded hurt feelings above all things.

"We found your flowers in our room Saturday night," she said, smiling. "They were very pretty, and we want to thank you for them."

"But you mustn't send any more," Polly put in, quite gently for her. "We really appreciate the thought, but— Well, you both know how easy it is for all the rest of the girls to cry— Crush—Crush."

"Oh, but we didn't, haven't," Jane and Phylis blurted out, "really, Polly."

"Of course you haven't a crush," Lois said, soothingly. "We know that you don't believe in them, or you would never have lectured Fanny so about sentimentality, yesterday."

Polly gasped; was Lois really sarcastic—personally—she preferred the direct attack.

"You know," she began firmly, "you had no right to talk that way to a Junior — it was disrespectful, and Fanny had a right to be angry."

Jane and Phylis hung their heads.

"I know it; we didn't really mean to be fresh," Jane said, apologetically. "We just thought maybe Fanny was homesick, and we'd cheer her up."

"We were going in to advise her who to vote for as captain, really," Phylis took up the tale, "but she wouldn't give us a chance. After we hinted that she shouldn't be boy crazy she sent us out. It doesn't really matter; she'll vote for you—" Phylis stopped. Tears of mortification came to her eyes. "Anyway," she finished, hastily, "we won't send you any more flowers, if you don't want us to, and, honestly, we won't have a crush."

Polly laughed good naturedly and put her arm around Phylis' shoulder.

"That's all right; we don't want you to; but, I'll tell you something. If you would really like to do something we would like—learn to play a good game of basket ball. You might be needed some day."

"Poll, what made you hold out hopes to those children?" Lois asked later, as they waited for their tubs to fill. They had played basket ball with some of the old girls after they had left Jane and Phylis.

"Because I thought they needed something to think about besides hurt feelings; I don't think they'll get their hopes up for the team."

"Well, you may have been right," Lois agreed slowly. "Anyway our little lecture did them good. Fanny stopped me after practice and told me they had apologized."

Polly said: "Oh, did they?" indifferently, and went to her tub to turn off the water.

Her head was in a whirl, and, suddenly, tempting hopes ran riot. She stood looking at the water a minute and shivered in anticipation of the plunge.

"Captain of the basket ball team," she whispered. "I wonder—"

CHAPTER IV
BASKET BALL ELECTION

As Senior President, Lois was a decided failure. It was not through any lack of interest on her part in the class and its affairs, but rather because the fairies at her christening had failed to bestow upon her the gift of leadership with which Polly was so richly endowed.

She just couldn't think of the hundred and one practical things that needed attending to. Perhaps Miss Crosby was partly to blame. She had taken a decided interest in Lois from their meeting on the stairs, and had given her permission to use the studio at any time. She had criticized her work and gave her helpful points not infrequently in her own room, where Lois often dropped in at tea time.

But progress in art, though beneficial to Lois, was of no use to the Senior class. Polly was at her wit's end. Lois had called a class meeting the day before and forgotten to come to it. School had been running smoothly for over a month by now, and all the strangeness of the first few weeks had worn off. With Thanksgiving in sight, the girls felt that they were well into the year.

To-day was Friday. After dinner the election for the basket ball captain was scheduled and nothing was arranged.

Polly, after looking in the gym and some of the classrooms for Lois, returned to Senior Alley. She was excited about the election, but she was more deeply concerned about Lois. She was thinking and she walked slowly in consequence. As she entered the corridor Dot Mead's voice, high pitched and angry, made her stop abruptly.

"Not a thing planned, the slips not ready, and here it is Friday afternoon. Lois wasn't like this last year. If she accepted the office of president why doesn't she act up to it! Why, even the Freshmen are criticizing." Her voice subsided into a grumble of displeasure.

Polly shook her head slowly and went quietly into her own room. The Dorothys were growling as usual. She had to admit that this time there was a little cause, too.

What had come over Lois. Polly realized with a sudden drawing together of her eyebrows, that she was seeing less and less of her all the time. "Art!" she said, aloud, and laughed. Then she went out to find Betty.

"Something's got to be done," she announced, when she found her with Angela, "and we've got to do it. Ange, you print the notice of the election in red ink, and put it on the bulletin board. And, Bet, you make the ballot box. There's a big square wooden box under my bed — you can cut a hole in it. I'll go and find Phylis and Jane and get them to help me tear up paper slips. They'll love it, and they'll keep quiet about it."

"What'll we tell the rest?" Angela asked. "They ought to appreciate our saving them this trouble, but they won't," she added dryly.

Polly hesitated a moment.

"We'll post a notice on the board for a meeting to be held at two fifteen," she said boldly.

"But it's three o'clock," Angela protested, but Betty understood.

"I'm ashamed of your deceit, Polly," she said with pretended scorn, adding: "It's a bully idea."

"No, it's not; I hate it; it's really a written fib, but— Well, I'd do a lot more than that for Lo," Polly answered.

"Do you mean put up the sign so that the other girls will think we had a meeting, and they didn't come?"

Angela was flabbergasted at the idea.

"Exactly."

"Oh, I see. They'll be awfully cross we didn't send for them, and I love the two Dorothys when they're mad. But, Poll, for goodness' sake give Lois a lecture; we don't want this to happen too often, one fib's enough," she finished with a yawn. "Now, I'll go paint the sign."

Jane and Phylis were only too anxious to help make the slips — hero worship shone from their eyes as they took the sample from Polly.

"Aren't you excited?" Phylis asked. "Landy, I'd be standing on my head if I thought—" She stopped and clapped her hand over her mouth.

Phylis' frank adoration really amused Polly. She found it very hard sometimes to face it with the proper Senior dignity. The excited little Freshman reminded her of herself at the same age. She almost wished the youngsters could make the sub team as she and Lois had done.

"I'm not excited, because I don't think I have much chance," she answered, which was exactly what both girls had expected her to say.

"Bring those slips down to my room when you've finished, and don't say that you helped, will you? It wouldn't do for any one to think that the Seniors had favorite helpers," she said as she left them.

After she had gone, Jane and Phylis locked their door and talked in whispers, while they worked.

Polly went down stairs, printed out the notice of the class meeting and pinned it on the bulletin board. She had an uncomfortably guilty feeling, tinged with pride and a certain amount of satisfaction when it was up. For it took real courage for Polly to lie, even for Lois. Then she went to Betty's room, helped her with the box and did several other things.

It was time to dress for dinner before she returned to her room. She was brushing her hair before the dresser when Lois burst in upon her.

"Polly!" she exclaimed. "Isn't this awful! I forgot about to-night and all the things there were to do. I was painting in the studio—oh, a duck of a picture, the corner of the house that you see from the window, and I forgot all about the time. What, under the sun, will I do?"

Polly's chance had come, and she had no intention of letting it escape her.

"Rather late to do anything, don't you think?" she asked indifferently, still brushing her hair.

Lois was taken by surprise. "But, Poll, you've got to help me," she begged, "think how furious the Dorothys will be."

"Can you blame them?" Polly held her brush in mid air. "As an organized and governing class we are rather a joke, and the Dorothys don't like to be laughed at," she finished, cuttingly.

This was too much for Lois. She had been working hard all afternoon over her picture and she was tired. She threw herself down on her bed and burst into tears.

"Polly," she sobbed, "don't act like that. I know I'm no good as a president. I'll resign to-night, only — oh, dear — " The rest was muffled in the pillow.

Polly made a start forward, stopped, made a last effort to be severe, and gave in.

"Lois, dear, don't," she pleaded, kneeling beside the bed, "don't cry any more, sit up and listen to me. Everything's all right." Lois dabbed at her eyes. "We've had a class meeting, the box is ready, the slips are fixed and the notice is up. We're supposed to have had a meeting, that is, I put a sign up that there'd be one at two-fifteen, only — " Polly hesitated. "I put it up at three o'clock. The Dorothys and Evelin and Helen will think we had it without them."

"Polly!" Lois was beginning to understand. "You deliberately did that to save me. You darling, I promise I'll resign to-night."

"Resign!" Polly stood up, a sparkle in her eye. "Lois Farwell, if you resign, I'll never, never speak to you again. I mean it."

Lois was apparently frightened into submission, for she said:

"All right, Poll, I won't." Very meekly.

That evening the two Dorothys were astonished and not a little put out with the ease with which the election was gone through with. They had seen the class meeting sign, and with Evelin and Helen accepted it without a doubt, which added considerably to Polly's discomfort.

Lois, now that she was really awake to the necessity, acted the part of senior president, and announced and directed, quite properly.

The votes were cast in the Assembly Hall. Each girl wrote the name of her choice for captain on a slip of paper and put it in the box. Then, all the girls

27

who had been on the big team the year before, with the assistance of the Seniors, counted the votes.

The whole thing on this particular evening was gone through with in deadly silence, which was nerve racking, particularly to Polly. Not for worlds would she have confessed what it meant to her, but ever since her Freshman year, she had wanted to be captain. She had condemned the wish as foolish, but she had continued to hope.

After what seemed an endless wait, the names were sorted and counted, written on a sheet of paper and presented to Lois. She looked at it, gave a shout of joy, jumped up from her seat, and then, remembering the two Dorothys' love of form, she said quietly: "I have the honor to announce that Polly Pendleton has won the election by a sweeping majority."

And so it happened—

When the school heard it a little later everybody said:

"Why, of course. We knew it; no one else had a chance," and hurried to Polly to congratulate her. She said: "Thank you" to them all, and tried hard to fight down the silly, but uncontrollable longing to cry.

Lois slipped away the very first chance she got and went down stairs. On her way she met Betty.

"Where are you going?" she demanded.

Lois smiled, mysteriously.

"To send a telegram to Bob," she answered. "He made me promise I would."

The next day at luncheon, Polly found a yellow envelope at her place at table.

"What under the sun!" she demanded, looking at it. "Who do you suppose it's from?"

"Opening it would be a good way to find out," Betty suggested.

Polly tore open the envelope.

"Why it's from Bob! Lois, you wretch, listen!"

And she read the message. "Lois wired me the good news. Hearty congratulations, and good luck. Bob."

"Don't call me a wretch." Lois protested, with a wicked grin. "Bob made me vow I'd wire him the minute little Polly was elected."

For the rest of the meal Polly was teased unmercifully.

After school the three held council, while she took down Lois' Princeton banner—for a week was up—and triumphantly put up her own.

"I don't envy you your job, Polly," Betty began, "who are you going to choose for your team?"

"Isn't it a blessing the Dorothys don't play?" Lois laughed, "or we'd have to have them."

"Why the main team is easy," Polly said. "There's you and Bet, and Evelin and myself already on it, and all Seniors; that only leaves two more to choose, and they'll have to be Juniors. Let's get Evelin and go over to the gym and see what's doing."

They found sweaters and caps, called Evelin, and started off. Angela met them on the way.

"I'm going, too," she insisted; "even if I can't play, my advice is invaluable."

When they reached the gym a game was under way, and much to their surprise, Fanny Gerard was in the thick of it.

"Jemima! look at that!" Betty exclaimed, as she made a difficult basket. "Now who'd have thought it!"

They had not seen much of Fanny in the last month. They had no idea she had taken their ridicule to heart. She had rebelled against it at first, and then, gradually, other interests had blotted out her resentment. Lately she had been playing basket ball every day.

Evelin was the only one of the girls watching who was not surprised.

"She's the right build," she said, "and I know she's been at it all the time— but, of course, she doesn't expect to make the team."

"She ought to. Look at that!" Lois drew attention to another play. "Imagine any one apparently as slow and dreamy as she is, playing such a rattling game. Let's put her down for a sub, anyway."

Polly, who had not been paying much attention to the rest, said suddenly:

"We'll have to put her on the main team. We need two girls, and there's only one other Junior besides Fanny who can play, and that's Eleanor Trent. She was on the team at the school where she went last year. There she is, the girl with the auburn hair. She's used to boys' rules, but otherwise she's a good player."

"Jemima! two new girls!" Betty said dolefully. "Well, it can't be helped. Certainly the old ones are a hopeless lot."

"When do we tell them?" Evelin inquired. "Let's do it now. Goodness! I remember how thrilled I was when I was put on last year."

"Let's call them out of the game; that'll make them feel so important," Lois suggested.

So Polly asked permission from Miss Stewart, the gym teacher, and Fanny and Eleanor came over to them.

Polly, as captain, told them they had been chosen for the big team. Eleanor had rather expected it. She was a good player, but she was delighted and promised to try and make good.

But Fanny! No words can express her excited raptures. She couldn't believe her good luck, and she sent the girls into peals of laughter by solemnly asking Polly to take her oath on it.

"I knew she'd be rare," Betty exclaimed on their way back to school. "I was sure she'd weep for joy."

"I hope it's all right," Lois said, doubtfully. "I wish she wasn't quite so excitable." Lois played basket ball with her head.

"Oh, she'll be all right if she doesn't go at it too hard," Polly said, assuringly. "Wonder if we have any mail?" She stopped before the Senior letter box. "One for you, Lo, from your mother, and one for me. Let's go in English room and read them. Mine's from Bob."

The other girls found their mail, and went up to their rooms.

Lois and Polly, left alone, opened their letters and read them through.

"Mother's is awfully short," Lois said, before Polly had finished hers. "She says she knows something awfully nice that's going to happen Thanksgiving, but she has promised Bob not to tell. What's yours about?"

"Oh, Lo! poor Bobbie has sprained his ankle and he can't run any more." Polly's voice trembled. "I'll read you what he says:

"Dear Old Polly:

"Telegraphing congratulations is no good. It costs too much to be eloquent. Besides, I've a lot of things I want to say, but, first of all, Three Cheers for you. Seddon Hall is darn lucky to have such a corking little captain—and you'll lead them to victory and have your name on the cup. Make them put it on extra large."

"Old tease," Polly laughed, and Lois said: "Just like Bob."

"And now, I'm going to talk about myself. Two weeks ago I sprained all the ligaments in my foot, and—well, there's not much use my trying to be cheerful about it—not to you anyway. It means I probably won't be able to run again—and so, good-by to my hopes of winning my H. Remember the long talks we used to have about it? I guess instead of watching me cross the tape from the grand stand, you'll sit beside me next May and listen to me groan while some other fellow runs in my place, which reminds me:

"I've planned a surprise for you and Lois on Thanksgiving. I don't like to boast, but it's rather nice—even mother says so.

"Drop me a line, Miss Basket Ball Captain, and tell me you'll accept.

"Yours,

"Bob."

"How exciting! What do you suppose it is?" Lois demanded, as she followed Polly upstairs. "It's a shame about Bobbie's foot. Vacation begins next week. Isn't it thrilling! I do hope he has sense enough to bring home some one nice—but I suppose it will be his roommate, Jim Thorpe, as usual, and I don't like him much." They had reached their room by now.

"I'll bet the surprise is a football game, don't you?" Lois persisted.

"Oh, keep still, Lo!" Polly said, crossly, "and leave me alone."

Lo glanced up in surprise, and suddenly decided to look for Betty. She left Polly standing before the Crimson banner, blinking hard.

CHAPTER V

THANKSGIVING

Thanksgiving vacation started with the confusion and excitement always necessary when a school breaks up even for so short a time.

Polly and Lois could hardly wait until the Seddon Hall special pulled into the Grand Central station on Wednesday morning. The vacation began on Wednesday and the girls were expected to be back Sunday evening.

They were the first to jump to the platform as the train stopped.

Mrs. Farwell was waiting for them.

"Darling children!" She hugged and kissed them both. "How well you look!"

"Well? Why we're robust, Aunt Kate," Polly laughed, "and bursting with excitement."

"What's the surprise, Mother? Please tell us," Lois begged.

Mrs. Farwell only shook her head mysteriously. "Not a word until after luncheon. We must shop this morning." She looked at the girls despairingly. "How do you manage to wear out your clothes so? You both need everything new, particularly hats; the ones you have on are sights."

Uncle Roddy's car was waiting for them, and they got in it and were whirled away to the shops.

It was not until luncheon that they had a chance to breathe.

"There, that's settled." Mrs. Farwell viewed them with satisfaction. She was proud of them both. Lois' delicate handsomeness and Polly's clear cut beauty. She had chosen dark blue for the one and hunter's green for the other.

"Won't you girls ever take an interest in your clothes?" she asked, wonderingly. She couldn't believe they were quite as indifferent to the charming pictures they made in the very becoming hats and sporty topcoats as they pretended.

"Poor, darling mother, we are interested," Lois protested, "but we're — "

"Fussed." Polly finished for her, looking decidedly self-conscious, as she tilted her hat a tiny bit more over one ear.

Uncle Roddy and Dr. Farwell met them for luncheon, and then they heard the plan.

"It's Bob's idea," Uncle Roddy explained, "and here's the schedule. You," he was looking at Polly and Lois, "and Mrs. Farwell leave for Boston this afternoon. Bob will meet you and take you to dinner, and to-morrow you'll go to the game. Harvard plays Princeton."

"That's hard on you, Lois," Dr. Farwell laughed; he never stopped teasing for one minute.

"What do you think about it, Tiddledewinks?" Uncle Roddy asked.

"It's a perfect plan," Polly said, enthusiastically. "I'm crazy to see Bob. Isn't it a shame about his foot?"

The doctor looked grave.

"Yes, it's too bad; he was laid up for quite a while. Of course, it's all right now, but he lost time, and he's had to make up a lot of work."

"Oh, of course." Polly suddenly realized that Bob's father was not looking at it from quite the same angle that she was.

After luncheon they hurried to the hotel where the Farwells were staying, repacked their bags and were back at the Grand Central in time for their train.

Lois and Polly talked and planned ahead all the way to Boston. They thoroughly enjoyed the coming fun in anticipation; but, of course, they never guessed for a second that the real surprise was still ahead.

"There's Bob," Polly exclaimed, as they followed the porter through the gates. "I can see him; he's way at the end of that line of people, and Lois, look who's with him!"

Lois looked. A tall, heavily set fellow, with a very broad pair of shoulders, was waving his hat.

"Frank Preston! Why how do you suppose—" But the rest of the sentence was cut short by the meeting.

"Hello, Mother!" Bob began, "how are you?" He turned to the girls. "Here's a friend of yours, Lo." Then he squeezed Polly's hand till it hurt.

"How do you do, Mrs. Farwell?" Frank shook hands hurriedly and turned to Lois.

"Isn't this bully luck? Gee, I'm glad to see you!" he said, eagerly.

Bob looked in admiration. He wished he had Frank's courage. Why he couldn't even kiss his mother and Lois in public, without blushing, and as for Polly, well, he would have to wait until they were alone before he could tell her how glad he was to see her. But he comforted himself with the thought that he'd be more artistic about it when the time came than Frank had been.

They found their hotel, the same one they had stayed at on their first memorable trip to Boston, and Mrs. Farwell, tired out from her strenuous afternoon, ordered tea at once.

Lois and Frank sat down on a sofa at one end of the room, and Frank explained how Bob had wired him to meet him.

"Of course, I came," he said.

"You are not in the game to-morrow?" Mrs. Farwell asked from behind the tea urn.

"No, worse luck," Frank told her. "I'm only a sub; of course, there's a chance; I may be needed."

"But if you're a sub, how did you manage to get here?" Polly inquired.

"Oh, I managed that all right. I won't break training, though I'm tempted to." He eyed the tea cakes longingly, "and I'll be on hand to-morrow. So that's all right. It's awfully jolly of you people to ask me," he smiled, engagingly, at Mrs. Farwell.

"Why, we're delighted to have you, Frank," she assured him.

Bob, who had been looking out of the window all this time, turned abruptly.

"Mother, Polly doesn't want any tea, and there's loads of time for a walk; do you mind?" he asked.

His mother laughed. "Not if Polly doesn't, but I should think she'd be tired."

But Polly was not tired. She insisted that she wanted some exercise after the trip on the cars. So Bob took her out.

The sun was just getting ready to set, and they walked towards the river.

"Polly!" Bob said, after they had walked a block in silence.

"Yes—"

"I think this is pretty much O. K., don't you?"

"What, this street?" Polly was very happy and she felt like teasing.

Bob tightened his grip on her arm, started to protest, and then changed his mind.

"Yes, of course, this street; I think it's a lovely street—in fact it's a great favorite of mine," he said instead.

Then Polly was sorry. After a while she said, softly:

"What did you really mean, Bobby?"

"Why, the street."

"Oh, very well, if you don't want to tell me."

"Ha, ha! but I do; I think it's great having you here for the game, and mother and Lois. Wasn't I clever to get Frank to amuse Lo to-night? We're going to the theater, you know, something musical. I wish he could stay longer, but, of course, he can't; he'll have to return with the defeated team."

"Will they surely be defeated?" Polly asked, seriously. "Bob, I think I'll just die if Harvard doesn't win."

"Don't worry, we will," he assured her with perfect confidence. Then followed another pause. They had reached the river, and Polly stopped.

36

"Bob!"

"What is it?"

"I'm awfully sorry about your foot; I can't tell you how sorry, because words are so stupid; the right ones never come when you really want to say something. But I feel about it, oh, awfully! Isn't there even a chance?"

"Yes, a little one," Bob said; "but not enough to matter. I can't start training, and I'll be too stiff to do any good by Spring.

"Tough luck!" Polly laid her hand unconsciously on his arm. "Don't give up, though. You may make good if you work awfully hard. May's ages off."

"Gee!" Bob delivered this inelegant exclamation with feeling. "Poll, you're the best little sport I ever knew. You always understand. Any other girl would have said that running was bad for my heart, and expected me to be consoled."

Polly was overcome by such frank praise. She tried to think of something to say, and finally decided on:

"Oh, rot! Isn't it time to go back?"

The theater that night was very amusing. Lois and Frank were in gales of laughter every minute.

"If you laugh any more," Lois said, between the acts, "you'll never be able to play to-morrow."

"But I won't have to play," Frank protested, "unless an awful lot of awful things happen. Anyway, don't let's talk about it, honestly, Lois." He lowered his voice, "I get cold all over when I think of it. I'm almost sure I'd lose my nerve if I had to go in."

"You never would," Lois admonished, crisply. "You'd find it, any amount of it, the minute you heard the signals. I hope — oh, how I hope you have to play."

"Well, if I do," Frank grumbled, "it won't do me any good to remember you're on the Harvard side."

"Now, you're silly," Lois teased. "What difference does it make where I sit, so long as I root for Princeton?"

"Do you mean that?" Frank demanded. "Do you honestly want us to win? Gee, that's great! I sort of thought, because of Bob—"

"Oh, Bob! Well, you see there's Polly," Lois said, demurely, just as the curtain rose for the last act.

Thanksgiving morning was all glorious sunshine. There was not a single cloud in the sky, and the air was just the right football temperature.

"Everything O. K., so far," Bob said, joyfully, as he joined his mother and the girls at breakfast. "What'll we do this morning to kill time?"

"Lois wants to go to the Library and see the Abbey pictures," Mrs. Farwell answered.

Bob looked his disgust—he appealed to Polly—but for the first time she deserted him.

"I'm going too, Bobby. I guess you'll have to find something to do until luncheon," she said.

Mrs. Farwell and the girls wandered about the Library all morning, and returned to the hotel ten minutes later than the time set by Bob for luncheon.

He and his roommate, Jimmy Thorpe, were waiting for them in the lobby.

"I knew you'd be late," Bob greeted them. "We'll have to dash through lunch. Did you enjoy the pictures?" he asked, sarcastically.

"Darling Bobby, are we late? We're so sorry. How do you do, Jimmy? It's awfully nice you can be with us." Mrs. Farwell was so contrite and charming that Bobbie's momentary huff disappeared as it always did before his mother's smile.

"Well, we didn't have to hurry so very much," she said, when luncheon was over and they were preparing to start. "Now are you sure we are going to be warm enough?"

Bob and Jim looked at each other, over the sweaters and steamer rugs they were loaded down with, and winked.

"Here's the taxi," Jim announced. "Come on, Lois."

After a considerable time lost in stopping and threading their way among the other hundreds of cars, they reached the Harvard Stadium at last.

"Bob, how wonderful and how huge it looks to-day," Polly exclaimed, as they entered their section, and she caught sight of the immense bowl, and the hundreds of people.

They had splendid seats, near enough to really see and recognize the players. Jim and Bob explained the score card, talked familiarly about all the players and pointed out the other under graduates who had won importance in other sports.

"Oh, but I wish I were a boy," Polly said, longingly. "Imagine the thrill of being part of all this. Why it makes school look pale and insignificant in comparison."

"I don't wish I were a boy," Lois said decidedly. "I'd much rather be a girl, but, I'll admit, football does make basket ball look rather silly."

"Oh, I don't know!" Jim said, condescendingly. "Basket ball's a good girls' game."

Polly was indignant.

"Jim, what a silly thing to say. You know perfectly well that just as many boys play it as girls. The only difference is that when we play we have to use our minds — while boys — "

"Yes, we know, Poll," Bob interrupted, "boys have no minds; therefore their rules must be less rigid. But don't be too hard on us."

"I judge Polly plays basket ball." It seemed to be Jim's day for blunders.

"Plays basket ball — oh, ye Gods!" Bob wrung his hands. "Why, Jim, surely I told you that she was no less than captain of her team. Personally, I think she deserves the title of general."

Polly laughed in spite of herself.

"Bob, you're a mean tease. But just wait. I'll ask you both up for field day, and—"

"Sh—! here they come," Bob warned as a prolonged cheer announced the arrival of the teams.

The game was on.

Everybody stood up and shouted. And then a tense silence followed, as the first kick-off sent the pigskin hurtling into the air.

Any one who has seen a football game knows how perfectly silly it is to attempt a description of it. Polly and Lois could both tell you all the rules and explain the most intricate maneuvers, if you gave them plenty of time to think it out; but with the actual plays before them, they were carried away by excitement and gave themselves up completely to feeling the game, rather than understanding it. They watched the massed formation with breathless anxiety, thrilled at every sudden spurt ahead which meant a gain; groaned when the advance was stopped by one of those terrifying tackles, and experienced the exultant joy only possible when the pigskin sails unchecked between the goal posts.

Between periods they had to appeal to Jim and Bob for the score. At one point in the game, Bob turned hurriedly to Lois.

"Watch out for Frank," he said, excitedly; "He'll be on in a minute."

"How do you know?" Lois demanded. "Oh, Bobby, I wish they wouldn't; he, he—said he'd lose his nerve." Lois had suddenly lost hers.

"You watch that man," Bob pointed, "they'll take him out, see if they don't; he's all in. Frank will play next period."

He was right. When the whistle blew, Frank, after a few hurried words with the coach, tore off his sweater and ran out to the field.

Lois' eyes were glued to him whenever he was in sight, and during one tackle when he was completely lost under the mass of swaying arms and legs, she forgot her surroundings and the fact, most important in Bob's and Jim's eyes, that she was on the Harvard side—by shouting lustily.

"Stop it, stop it! Get off, you'll smother him!"

Mrs. Farwell quieted her.

"Lois, you mustn't, dear child," she laughed. "They can't hear you, you know. Do sit down and don't look if it frightens you."

By this time Frank was up and doing wonders. Lois gave a sigh of relief.

"Football's a savage game," she said, indignantly. And Mrs. Farwell agreed with her. She had been thankful beyond words that Bob had not gone out for the team—running was sufficiently dangerous. It was to her lasting credit that she had thought of Bob's feelings first, instead of her own, when news came of his hurt foot.

Putting Frank in the game made a decided difference. The Orange and Black began to gain. They fought and contested every inch, but the Crimson triumphed.

Polly's eyes reflected the light of victory as the last longed for whistle blew. She shouted and went quite mad with all the rest.

"What a game! Oh, Bob, what a game!" she cried as they started for their exit. "I'll never be able to thank you enough for taking me. I'm nearly dead from excitement, though."

Bob, in his exuberance, slapped her on the back.

"Good for you, Polly; you ought to have been a boy, shouldn't she, Jim?" he demanded.

"Why, I can't see that there's any room for improvement, if you ask me," Jim said gallantly. And Bob gnashed his teeth.

They all had dinner at the hotel that night, and went to the theater again, but it is a question whether any of them could tell you what they saw, for the music acted only as a sort of fitting background as they went over and over again, each play of the wonderful game.

That is, Polly and Bob and Jim. Lois had only one comment to make:

"Princeton lost," she granted them, "but it was only because they hadn't the sense to put Frank in sooner." And Bob admitted there might be a degree of truth in what she said.

CHAPTER VI

MAUD

The rest of Thanksgiving vacation was so pale in comparison with the game that it is not worth recounting. Only one thing of lasting importance occurred.

Sunday morning, while Lois and Polly were still in bed—Lois was staying with Polly at Uncle Roddy's apartment on Riverside Drive—the bell rang. Mrs. Bent the housekeeper opened the door and Mrs. Farwell walked in.

"Good morning," she said hurriedly—and catching sight of Mr. Pendleton in the library—added, "I know I'm much too early for dinner, Roddy—the doctor said you wouldn't be up, but I have such exciting news for the girls. Where are they?"

"Still in bed. I think they're having breakfast. You might go see. Tell me about the excitement first," Uncle Roddy answered, as he helped her with her coat.

"I found a letter from Mrs. Banks, when I got home from the theater last night," Mrs. Farwell explained. "It had been forwarded from Albany. They are back from Canada."

"The Banks, eh! How is Maud?" Uncle Roddy inquired with sudden interest.

"Very well, and Mrs. Banks wants to send her—but I must tell the girls," she interrupted herself, and hurried down the hall.

The Banks need a word of explanation to those who have not read the story of the first summer that Polly and Lois spent in the former's old home in New England, where they lived in Polly's own house left to her by her Aunt Hannah Pendleton. It was a big, rambling place and quite a distance from the village. The only other house on the hill was the mysterious Kent place—said by the natives for miles around—to be haunted.

It was with the greatest surprise that Polly, on her arrival, learned that this summer it was tenanted by a Mrs. Banks and her daughter, Maud. But instead of the occupants completely dispelling the mystery of the house, the Banks added to it.

It was soon evident, that there was something queer about them. Maud was very shy, and more like a frightened, wild animal, than a healthy, normal child. It was Dr. Farwell, who, towards the end of the summer, discovered that she was suffering from a severe nervous shock, caused by the tragic death of her father in India.

He had sent her away for treatment and when she returned, Polly and Lois had tried to complete the cure. Polly had almost succeeded in persuading her to return with them to Seddon Hall, but Maud's timidity had barred the way. She could not make up her mind to face the one hundred girls.

Mrs. Banks had taken her daughter to Canada to visit friends that winter, and apart from an occasional postal, Polly and Lois had heard no further news of them.

Mrs. Farwell's letter was a great surprise. When she entered the girl's room they both sat up. They had finished breakfast and were just being happily lazy.

"Jemima! What time is it?" Lois demanded, at sight of her mother. "Are you and Daddy here for dinner already?"

Mrs. Farwell laughed. "No, you lazy bones, it's not quite as late as that. I came before Daddy, because I have news for you—such news!"

"Tell us," Polly demanded, quite thoroughly awake. "News of what?"

Mrs. Farwell sat down on the edge of the bed and began:

"I've had a letter from Mrs. Banks, she and Maud are in New York and—"

But the girls interrupted her with a flood of questions.

"Mrs. Banks in New York! How's Maud? Did she say where she was going to school?"

"Is she still so awfully nervous?"

"I wonder what she's like now."

"Do listen," Mrs. Farwell begged, "and I'll tell you. Mrs. Banks wrote that she was considering sending Maud to Seddon Hall. She is fifteen now, you know, and apparently, from what her mother writes — eager to go."

Polly said: "Well, I never! It's taken her two years to make up her mind."

Lois groaned, and fell back on her pillows. You will remember, she was never as interested in Maud, as Polly was.

"Another younger girl to look after," she said dolefully. "I wonder if there'll be room for her. When are you going to answer Mrs. Banks' letter, mother?"

Mrs. Farwell thought for a minute.

"Why I think I'll 'phone her. You see the letter was sent to Albany, so it was delayed in reaching me. I have their address here."

"Look!" Polly bounded out of bed. "Call her up now Aunt Kate, and ask her to bring Maud to tea this afternoon. Then we can talk about school and see Maud. Get up, Lo, and do show a little interested enthusiasm," she admonished, as Mrs. Farwell went back to the library to tell Uncle Roddy the rest of the story, and to 'phone to Mrs. Banks. "Aren't you excited?"

"No!" Lois got up slowly and struggled to find her slipper. "I am not," she said slowly but distinctly.

Mrs. Banks was delighted to accept Mrs. Farwell's invitation, and at four o'clock they arrived, she and Maud.

The girls could hardly restrain a gasp of surprise at the sight of Maud. It is hard to realize that other girls grow up as well as yourself, and Polly and Lois still remembered the shy little girl in a pinafore, with straight flaxen hair and blue eyes that Maud had been two summers before. They were totally unprepared to meet the new Maud.

In the first place, instead of looking down at her they had to look up, for she had grown until she was a half head taller than either Polly or Lois. Her arms and legs were lanky and her hair was now brushed severely back from her forehead and hung in a heavy braid down her back. She wore a very plain black velvet dress with a broad white collar and cuffs, and with her clear blue eyes and straight features she made a strikingly handsome picture, and although she spoke in her same soft melodious voice — all trace of shyness was gone. After the greetings were over, and everybody was comfortably settled, the talk turned to school.

"Where have you been the past two years?" Polly asked. "I'm so tickled to think you've really decided to go to Seddon Hall at last."

"I've had governesses, most of the time," Maud answered.

"But you went to a small private school too, dear," Mrs. Banks reminded her.

Maud glanced at her mother and then back to Polly.

"Not for long, though; you see I was expelled," she said, with such unexpected bluntness, that they all laughed.

"Expelled! What for?" Lois asked, without intending to be rude.

"For drawing a picture of the music professor. It wasn't a very flattering picture, so!"

"You weren't really expelled, dear," Mrs. Banks said apologetically. "The Principal just thought you might be happier somewhere else. You didn't fit in; you see it was a very small school, and — "

"All the girls were little gentlewomen," Maud interrupted, without appearing rude, "and I was too noisy." She chuckled to herself — probably at the memory of past pranks. "I didn't mean to be, but the Principal — " She stopped abruptly. She was a little embarrassed at so much undivided attention — for though she was noisy, and rather unmanageable, she had no desire to show off. For the rest of the visit, the older people did the talking.

An hour later, as the girls were packing their bags, in Polly's room — they discussed Maud. It was decided that she was to go to Seddon Hall as soon as Mrs. Banks could arrange with Mrs. Baird, and the girls were wondering just what difference her coming would make.

"She'll be some one anyway," Polly said thoughtfully, "Whether she's popular or not, she's sure to make herself felt."

"I think she'll make a hit," Lois replied, slowly. "She's awfully different. I wonder if she'll start drawing pictures of the faculty."

"It doesn't matter if she does, no one will pay any attention to it," Polly said, with a grin. "Maybe she'll put some ginger into things."

"Bet will be pleased if she does," Lois laughed, as she packed her football score card. The sight of it made her exclaim:

"Poll, I meant to write Frank to-day! I haven't congratulated him yet. We've been so busy." She hurried to the desk. "I'll have time to tear off just a line before we start."

Polly was suddenly reminded of an unanswered letter at the same time. In a second their pens scratched in unison, and Maud was completely forgotten.

CHAPTER VII
A SENIOR DISPUTE

The last bell was three minutes late in ringing. Betty knew it was, because she had watched the clock tick out each one with growing impatience. When it did ring at last, she threw her latin book into her desk, banged down the lid, and gave vent to her favorite exclamation.

"Jemima! Thank goodness that's over." She went to the window and looked out.

A heavy snow had been falling all morning, and the grounds of Seddon Hall were sufficiently covered to assure good coasting.

Polly finished the last couple of sentences of her latin prose with little or no regard to the context and joined Betty.

"Looks bully, doesn't it?" she asked. "I hope it stays long enough to pack."

"It's wonderful," Betty agreed, "but don't let's stand and look at it any longer. Come on out, quick."

"Coming, Lo?" Polly inquired, stopping beside Lois' desk.

"No, not just yet. I've got to speak to Miss Crosby, over in the studio. Don't wait for me. I'll come as soon as I can," she promised. As she saw Polly's look of disapproval, adding by way of apology, "I simply must finish that sketch, Poll. It won't take long."

So Polly and Betty left her and went out together. They found their sleds from the year before, in the gym cellar, and pulled them to the top of the hill.

The snow had drifted into the road, and was so deep that the coasting was slow at first.

"Let's wait awhile," Betty suggested, "until the other girls have packed it down a little; this is no fun."

"All right, let's take a walk. I wish I knew how to snowshoe," Polly said as she sank to her knees in a drift.

"When's that friend of yours coming?" Betty inquired, as they started off towards the pond.

"Who, Maud? I don't know, sometime soon. We've got to be good to her, Bet. She's really all right in some ways."

"I remember her only that first summer," Betty said thoughtfully. "She didn't make much of an impression then."

"Did you ever see her ride?" Polly demanded. "We used to go out in the back pasture and try and tame a couple of colts we had. Maud was a wonder. Perhaps Mrs. Baird knows when she's coming."

"Let's go ask her." Betty turned back toward the school. "My feet are soaked anyway."

Mrs. Baird was standing on the Senior porch when they came up the drive. She called to them.

"Did Jane find you?" she asked, as they reached the steps. "I sent her to look for you."

Polly laughed. "Why no," she said surprised. "We were just coming to find you."

"What about?" Mrs. Baird put an arm around each girl. "Come inside, first," she said, shivering, for she was without hat or coat.

"Perhaps it was about the same thing," Betty said. They followed her into the office and Polly asked:

"Have you heard anything from Mrs. Banks? We're wondering when Maud is coming."

"To-morrow, and I meant to tell you and Lois, but it slipped my mind," Mrs. Baird told her.

"Then you wanted us for something else?" Betty asked.

Mrs. Baird walked over and looked out of the window.

"Yes," she said, hesitating. "I am worried about the coasting this year. We have so many new girls and I don't want any accidents. Of course I couldn't forbid them to coast, so I thought up a scheme. You two girls have been here for a long time and know all about the hill. By the way, where's Lois?" she asked abruptly.

"Up in the studio," Polly said with a shrug of her shoulders, which meant to convey the idea that Lois had taken up her permanent abode there.

Mrs. Baird frowned. "She must not work so hard," she said, finally. "She should be out on such a glorious day. I'll speak to her about it."

"Oh, she'll come out in a little while," Betty hastened to say. "She's just talking to Miss Crosby."

"Oh, well! I'll leave you two to see that she does," Mrs. Baird said severely. "And now, about the coasting. I want you three girls, and any of the other Seniors, of course,"—she added, on second thought—"to watch every new girl go down the hill once, then if she is really not fit to coast, you must tell her. I'll leave the decision to you."

"You mean that if we don't think they really know enough about it, that we are to tell them they must keep off the big hill?" Polly asked. The idea struck her as a very good one—new girls were always a nuisance at first—but she wished the decision had been left to some one else.

"They can use the little hill, can't they?" Betty asked. "No one could hurt themselves on that."

Mrs. Baird nodded her head. "That I leave to you; you're much the better judge. Only do make haste, I am so afraid some one will be hurt. I saw little Phylis Guile almost run into a tree."

Polly and Betty promised to start at once. They went up to the studio and made Lois put away her brushes and join them. Then they told the Dorothys and Evelin and Mildred. Polly stationed them along the hill— Betty at the top, to judge of the start—the others along the way, while she and Lois watched the curve at the end.

They stayed at their posts all the afternoon, every now and then jotting down some girl's name and quietly telling them that they would have to do the rest of their coasting on the little hill. Sometimes they met with protests, but, for the most part their Senior dignity upheld them.

"What under the sun will we do about Jane and Phylis?" Polly asked. "They'll kill themselves if they go down again, and if we just tell them they can't it will break their hearts."

Lois considered. "I've got it. We'll make it seem a favor to us."

"But how?" Polly demanded, as the two younger girls came flying recklessly around the turn.

"Leave that to me," Lois whispered. "Oh, Jane, will you and Phylis come here a minute? Polly and I have the greatest favor to ask of you. I wonder if you'll help us out?" she asked.

"Of course we will," they answered promptly. "We'll do anything."

Lois felt like a hypocrite, but she went on to explain:

"It's about coasting," she said. "You see, Mrs. Baird has asked us to tell all the new girls that are not used to such a dangerous hill, that they must coast on the small hill by the pond. Of course some of them are not even able to do that, and they ought to be watched." Lois stopped — took a long breath and looked appealingly at Polly.

"We thought you might be willing to go over and coast there, and sort of keep an eye out that no one is hurt," Polly said, coming to her rescue. "We'll be so busy here."

"Why we'd love to," Jane said eagerly.

"We don't mind a bit," Phylis protested. "Are we to tell them to stop if we see any one that's reckless?"

"Mercy! No!" Lois exclaimed. She had a sudden vision of these two youngsters using their authority at every possible excuse. "That would hurt their feelings. Just use lots of tact and perhaps show them what to do, but not in a — in a — "

"I know," laughed Jane. "You mean don't be fresh the way we were to Fanny. We won't."

"Oh," Polly sighed when they had hurried off. "What a wonder you are, Lois, and they really will help."

"Of course they will. Good gracious! Here comes Fanny."

From where they stood they could see the long stretch of the hill, just before the curve. Fanny, sitting bolt upright, an unforgivable sin—in Polly's eyes—was whirling down it. She had apparently lost all control of her sled. Polly and Lois held their breath.

On one side of the curve, a big rock jutted out at right angles to the road, and on the other a cobble stone gutter offered almost as dangerous an alternative. Fortunately, Fanny, or rather Fanny's sled, chose the latter. There was a second of flying snow mixed up somehow with Fanny's arms and legs, and then quiet. Polly and Lois dashed to the spot.

"Are you hurt?" Lois demanded.

Fanny sat up. "Well I never did," she said wonderingly. "What do you suppose happened to that little old sled?"

Polly's sudden relief took the form of anger.

"You had no right to try this hill," she said severely. "Did Betty see you start?"

Fanny stiffened. "Yes, she did if you want to know," she said. "And she told me not to. But—" She paused to give her words better effect. "Betty and you and Lois are not the only Seniors at this school, though you do act most mighty like you thought you were. I got my permission from the two Dorothys," she finished with a triumphant toss of her head.

Polly and Lois looked at each other in amazement. Something had come over Fanny of late. They had noticed it, but other matters had made it seem unimportant. She had always been on hand for basket ball practice, but her attitude had been sullen and she had spent most of her time with the Dorothys and Evelin.

Polly realized that this was an important point and must be dealt with. She wasn't angry at Fanny, for she knew to just what extent her classmates were to blame.

"Did Dot Mead know Betty had told you not to coast on this hill?" she asked finally.

"She certainly did." Fanny was still triumphant.

Polly bit her underlip and half closed her eyes. Lois saw these unmistakable signs of danger, and tried to make peace.

"Are you sure?" she asked hopefully.

"I am." Fanny was ridiculously solemn.

"Then the Dorothys went beyond their authority," Polly said coldly. "And their permission counts for nothing. You can see for yourself that you can't manage on this hill; you nearly hurt yourself just now."

"I did no such a thing," Fanny interrupted lamely. But Polly paid no attention to her.

"As captain of the basket ball team, and Senior head of athletics" — the title rolled from her lips importantly — "I forbid you to coast on this hill again, no matter who gives you permission," she said with unmistakable decision. Then, without another word she turned on her heel and went up the hill with Lois.

Half way to the top, they found Betty in heated argument with Dot Mead. Now when Betty was angry she stormed. At this present moment, she was more than angry, she was furious.

"You had no right whatever to do it," she raged, as Polly and Lois joined them. "You didn't do it because you thought Fanny really knew how to coast; you just thought it was a good chance to get even with me. You've a fine idea of class dignity to do anything so petty. If you ever do a thing like that again — Jemima, I'll— You ought to be ashamed of yourself. You're jealous. That's—"

"Steady, Bet," Polly said quietly, "and do save your breath. Dot can't do it again. I've just told Fanny she must not use this hill and she quite understands."

"Then we will tell her she can." Dorothy Lansing spoke for the first time.

Betty and Lois looked at Polly. She picked up the rope of her sled and started up the hill.

"Tell her anything you like," she said over her shoulder, "but she won't coast again."

When the three reached Senior Alley, they met Angela. They were full of indignation and would have told her all about it, but Angela had news too. She greeted them excitedly.

"Girls! what do you think, Connie comes to-night. She'll be here on the five-eleven. She 'phoned Mrs. Baird from New York. Did you ever hear anything so thrilling? Just imagine Connie back again!"

"For good?" Polly demanded.

"No, just for a visit, she's going back day after to-morrow."

"Jemima! I'm glad," Betty exclaimed. "Won't it be natural to have her around again?"

"We've always missed her," Lois added. "Can't we have something special for her to-night?"

"How about a straw ride?" suggested Betty; "Mrs. Baird would let us—it's Friday."

"Oh, let's, and just ask the old girls who knew her," Angela hurried on—her drawl for once discarded. "We'll get Mrs. Baird to chaperone, if we can."

"I'll go ask her," Betty volunteered. "You go get the girls.

"I suppose all the Seniors will go," Angela said, none too enthusiastically, and Polly and Lois suddenly remembered that she had not heard about the Dorothys. Lois told her.

"Polly just mounted her dignity and oh, Ange, it was rare," she finished, laughing. "But I suppose they must be asked."

"Let's tell Bet she has to do it," Polly suggested. "She's so raging at Dot Mead, that she wants to box her ears."

"You'll really have to, Ange," Lois said.

"Not I, you're Senior president," Angela protested, adding nonchalantly: "Besides, if I ask, they might accept. Were Evelin and Helen in it?"

"No, they must go to-night; the Senior class must not be divided equally against itself," Polly said, thoughtfully. "I'll ask them now, and I'll make them go." She went off to find them.

A few minutes before study hour they all met in Study Hall.

"Mrs. Baird says we may go, of course," Betty began, "and she's told McDonald to bring around the sleigh at seven-fifteen."

"Will she chaperone?"

"No, she's got an awful lot to do. She suggested Miss Crosby. So I asked her. She said she'd love to— I'd rather have had Miss Porter, on account of Connie—but I didn't like to say so."

"Evelin and Mildred will come; they were a little cold at first," Polly said, "but they're all right now, and crazy to see Connie."

"How about the Dorothys, Lo?" Betty demanded.

Lois chuckled wickedly.

"They have made other plans for this evening, and will be unable to go," she said, sadly. "I didn't urge them."

"Good; that leaves about fifteen—just the right number for the wagon." Angela consulted her list. "I've got enough crackers and chocolate for everybody," she added.

"Look at the time!" Betty exclaimed. "Who keeps study hour to-night?"

"The Spartan."

"Oh, Lordy! Well, I'll have to be late. Somebody tell her I have Mrs. Baird's permission, if she misses my smiling face."

"Where are you going?" Polly asked.

"To get my clothes and take them to the guest room. Mrs. Baird said Connie would sleep with Ange while she's here. I'm off."

"Betty, you darling!" Angela exclaimed—but Betty was half way down the hall.

CHAPTER VIII

AN EVENTFUL STRAW-RIDE

Study hour began at five o'clock and lasted until six-thirty.

The girls found it impossible to get to work. At exactly five-eleven, Angela threw a note to Polly.

"Her train is due," it read. "Do you suppose we'll have to wait until dinner to see her?"

Polly shrugged her shoulders and shook her head in reply, and tried to get interested in her history.

A few minutes later, Lois left her seat and went over to the dictionary by the window. The sound of carriage wheels made her completely forget the word she was hunting for. She peeked out of the window. There was Connie on the driveway. Lois watched her pay the driver and pick up her suitcase. Then she went back to her seat.

"She's here," she whispered to Angela and Polly in passing.

Angela almost shouted with joy, but the Spartan's frown of displeasure at the disturbance at the back of the room made her bury her head in her desk. Just as the clock struck the half hour, Betty came in. She went up to the platform and said, loud enough for everybody to hear:

"Miss Hale, Constance Wentworth is here, and Mrs. Baird wants Angela in her office."

There was a general murmur of "oh, good!" through the room, and Angela was half way to the door before Miss Hale had given her permission. Everybody laughed as they heard her running down the stairs, two steps at a time.

Connie was waiting for her. They fell into each other's arms and kissed heartily. Mrs. Baird was sitting at her desk.

"Take Constance upstairs, will you, Angela," she said, smiling. "I'll excuse you from study hour, for I know you wouldn't be able to do any real studying. Constance will room with you. Betty has arranged it. Isn't it nice to have her back?" she asked with a special smile for Connie.

Tears, the sudden, grateful kind, sprang to Constance's eyes.

"Oh, if you knew how homesick I get for all this," she said falteringly. "I was afraid to come back for fear I'd feel out of it, but I don't," she added happily.

Angela took her bag and hurried her up to their room.

"Now, tell me all about everything," she demanded when Connie had taken off her things. "Don't you like the Conservatory?"

"Of course, it's wonderful," Connie answered, enthusiastically, "and I'm working like mad. I get awfully lonesome when I don't. How's everybody? I saw Bet for a second; she hasn't changed much."

"Everybody's fine. Lo saw you coming, and nearly jumped out of the window with excitement," Angela told her. "I've written you all the news. We're going on a straw-ride to-night—just the old girls that you know and like."

"Oh, fine! I hoped we could coast anyway." Connie was delighted. "Honestly, Ange," she said, seriously. "You don't know how good it is to stop being grown up. I have to be so dignified and ancient all the time, especially when I give concerts. Oh, by the way! I've got a surprise for you."

"What?" Angela demanded.

"I'm going abroad next spring to study for a year— I've won a scholarship."

"Connie! Not honestly?"

"Yes, it's all decided; mother is going to take me over and leave me; it's a secret, so don't tell any one."

Angela studied her friend's familiar face in silence for a minute. It was just like Connie to win a scholarship and then not tell anybody.

56

"I don't believe it's a secret," she said at last. "You just don't want anybody to know about it. Well, I'm going to announce it to the whole school," she finished grandly.

"Don't you dare, Ange. I'd die of embarrassment," Connie pleaded. "Promise you won't."

"I'll promise nothing," Angela insisted. "There's the bell. Come on and see Poll and Lo."

It was almost a marvel the way Angela followed out her threat. In the ten minutes before dinner, while Connie was surrounded by her other friends, she managed to convey to every girl in the school that Constance Wentworth was the most wonderful pianist in the world, and that she had, by her superior ability, won a scholarship.

Poor Connie! She was always shy where her music was concerned, and she blushed in misery under the torrent of congratulations, and never touched a bite of dinner.

At seven-fifteen the sleigh was waiting at the door. It was filled with fresh straw, and every available robe and blanket that could be found in the stables had been brought.

Old McDonald, one of the chief characters of Seddon Hall, sat on the front seat, muffled up to his eyes. He had grown quite old and feeble in the last two years, and many of his duties had been given to younger men, but no one thought of even offering to drive in his place to-night. He always drove the young ladies on their straw-rides, and he would never have even considered trusting them to the care of another.

Polly and Lois came out first, to be followed by Betty, and Angela and Connie.

They all got in and began sorting the robes — all but Polly — she went around to the horses' heads.

"Good evening, McDonald," she called. "Why, aren't these new?" She looked surprised at the splendid gray team — she had expected to see the two old bays.

"Yes, Miss Polly; they were bought last summer. The others were getting old and we put them out to pasture. How do you like this pair?"

"Why, they're beauties." Polly stroked their velvety noses, affectionately. "Are they frisky?"

"Well!" McDonald took time to think, "they are a bit, but nothing to be afraid of. I can manage them."

"Oh, of course you can!" Polly said, with so much conviction that the old man beamed with pride.

"All in!" Betty called, "and all aboard! Move your foot, Lo. I want one side of Connie."

"Where are we going?" somebody asked.

"Out towards Eagle's Nest," Polly answered. "The roads are not used out there and it ought to be good for sleighing."

"We're off."

"Cheer once for Seddon Hall," Betty commanded and was promptly obeyed. "Now for Connie. We've time for one song before we reach the village," she said, after Connie had been lustily cheered. "Everybody sing."

They reached the foot of the hill, and the horses broke into a quick trot— the bells on their harness jingled merrily in the crisp, cold air. It was a wonderful night. The moon was almost full, and its brilliant rays, falling on the white snow, made it sparkle like millions of stars.

"Are you quite comfy, Miss Crosby?" Lois asked. "There's a rug around here, somewhere, if you're cold."

"Thanks! I don't need it; I'm as warm as toast. My feet are lost somewhere in the straw. I feel as if I were back in Alaska again," Miss Crosby said, "only the horses should be dogs."

"Were you ever in Alaska?" half a dozen voices asked at once. The song was over and they were just entering the village.

"Tell us about it," Lois said.

"No, no, go on and sing some more!"

"We can't, not for a mile—that's a rule," Betty told her. "Mrs. Baird doesn't think the village people would appreciate our music," she explained. "They're not very nice people, but we can't annoy them. Please tell us about 'straw-rides in Alaska.'"

Miss Crosby laughed, and began. She was a charming woman and a gifted story-teller. She had traveled all over the world, and because she was interested in all the little things, her adventures had been many. She told them to-night about one ride she had taken for miles inland and held every one of them spellbound by her account of it.

They were far beyond the village before she stopped. "We finally did get to camp, and, of course, after it was over, it didn't seem so terrible," she finished. "Now do sing some more; you've made me talk quite long enough."

"And did the dog's foot get well?" Polly inquired, still miles away in fancy.

"No; he died," Miss Crosby whispered. "Plucky little fellow! Do sing."

There was a whispered consultation, and then:

"There's a teacher on our faculty, her name it is Miss Crosby," Betty sang, and the rest joined in the refrain: "Oh, we'd like to know any one with more go, and we will stand by her to the end-o." From one song they went to another, until they reached Eagle Nest.

"Everybody out!" Polly ordered, "and stretch. Where's that chocolate you were talking about, Ange? I'm hungry."

For five minutes they walked around, stamped their feet to warm up, munching crackers and chocolate in between.

Then McDonald called: "You've all got to come back, young ladies. I'm sorry, but these horses do hate to stand even a minute." He was very apologetic, but the grays were showing signs of restlessness, and pawing the ground.

The girls scrambled back into the sleigh and almost before they were seated the horses broke into a run.

About a mile farther on, as McDonald slowed down at a cross-road, they heard the jingling of other sleigh bells.

"Who do you suppose that is?" Connie asked. "Listen, they're singing!" A minute later a sleigh like their own swung round the corner — it was full of boys. Their driver slowed down to give McDonald the right of way.

"Why, it must be the Seddon Hall girls," they heard one of the boys shout. "Let's give them a cheer, fellows!"

"What school is it?" Miss Crosby asked. "Do you know, Lois!"

"Perhaps it's the Military Academy," Angela suggested.

Betty stood up in the middle of the sleigh and balanced herself by holding on to Connie and Lois.

"No!" she said. "They haven't any uniform on. I can see — I wish McDonald would let them get ahead."

By this time the yell was in full swing. When it ended the boys waited in vain for a reply.

"Maybe they didn't hear us," one of them shouted. "Let's give them a regular cheer with horns."

Polly, who had been edging up slowly toward the front seat of the sleigh, ever since they had started, gave a sudden spring and climbed up beside McDonald. She knew exactly what was going to happen.

At the first sound of the horn, the horses — already frightened out of their senses by all the singing and yelling — reared up on their hind legs for one terrifying second, and then bolted. Poor McDonald tried to bring them back under his control, but as he realized their condition, his nerve failed him.

"They're gone, Miss," he said in an agonized whisper to Polly, and his hands relaxed on the reins.

The girls, now thoroughly conscious of their danger, hung on for dear life, and some of them cried out.

The deafening shouts and the blowing of the horns kept up in the sleigh behind. The boys thought they were being raced.

Polly thought hard for just the fraction of a minute. Then she took the reins from McDonald's unresisting hands and pulled. She knew that her strength was not equal to stopping those wild runaways, but she felt she could keep them headed straight, and avoid tipping the sleigh. Just as she was trying to remember where she was and to place the hill that she knew was on the right at a cross-road, poor old McDonald fainted and fell backwards into the sleigh.

She didn't dare turn her head, but she heard Lois say:

"I've got him; help me, Bet," and Miss Crosby cry out:

"The reins! The reins!"

"I've got them; don't worry!" Polly's voice sounded miles away. Her head was throbbing. "Can I make it? Can I make it?" she kept saying over and over under her breath.

She saw the cross-road ahead; on the right a steep hill led up to an old, deserted hotel. For a minute she hesitated. The horses were good for miles more at top speed. She knew if they had level ground, that meant entering the village. She decided quickly. It must be the hill. If she could only make the turn. She tightened her grip on the reins and felt the horses slack just the least little bit. She pulled hard on the left rein, and then as they came to the turn — on the right one — so as to describe a wide half circle and save the sleigh from tipping. The sudden turn frightened the girls.

"Where are we going?"

"Oh, stop them!"

Polly heard their cries as in a dream. She took time to smile and toss her head to get a lock of hair out of her eye. She had felt the slight, but certain relaxing on the lines, and she knew the worst was over.

The hill was about a mile long, and by the time the horses reached the top, Polly had them completely under her control. She stopped them, finally, under the old tumbled down porte-cochère of the hotel. They were trembling all over and they were sweating.

"Get out!" Polly ordered, "and don't make any noise. We'll have to wait a minute before we go back—give me some blankets for the horses, and look after McDonald."

Miss Crosby was already doing it. The old man had collapsed and lost consciousness, but now he was coming around. With Betty to help, she had rolled him up in a robe in the middle of the sleigh, and tried to soothe him; his grief was pathetic.

"I'm done for; I'm done for!" he kept repeating.

Lois helped Polly with the horses.

"Sit down, Poll," she said, authoritatively. "You need rest, too. You'll have to drive us home."

Polly looked at her gratefully—her knees were trembling.

"I better keep going," she answered. "Just don't let the girls talk to me and I'll be all right." She was stroking one of the horse's necks.

Lois went round to the back of the sleigh. The girls were standing in a huddled group.

"Lo, will we ever get home?" Angela asked, tearfully.

"Of course, silly," Lois replied, calmly. "Polly stopped the horses running away; I guess she can drive us back all right; she's nervous, of course, so don't talk to her."

"We won't," Mildred said. "Mercy, but she's a wonder! I'm, oh! I'm going to cry."

Lois left the others to deal with her and returned to Polly.

"When do we start?" she asked, abruptly. Don't think for a minute she was acting under her natural impulse. If she had been, she would have thrown her arms around Polly and been very foolish; but she was trying to act the way she knew Bob would have—without fuss. She knew how Polly hated a fuss.

"Now, the horses mustn't catch cold and McDonald ought to see a doctor," Polly said. "Tell them to get in, will you? and, Lo," she added with a grin, "pray hard going down hill. I have my doubts about the brake."

When they were all in, Miss Crosby said:

"I think we better take McDonald to the hospital."

Polly nodded: "All right, I know where it is."

The horses, sure of themselves by now, and confident in their driver, behaved very well.

At the outskirts of the village, they drew up before the little white hospital, and Betty jumped out and rang the bell. A nurse answered it. In a few minutes they were carrying McDonald in on a stretcher.

As they started up the steps with him, he called: "Miss Polly!" in a shaky voice.

Polly jumped down from her seat, and went to him.

"I'm done for," he said, slowly, "and you're a very wonderful girl. You stopped those horses, you did, and I— I couldn't—" He broke down.

"Nonsense, McDonald! Your hands were cold," Polly said. "You'll be fine in the morning and able to drive anything. Cheer up!" But McDonald only repeated: "I'm done for."

A lump rose in Polly's throat at his distress, and she leaned down and kissed his wrinkled old face.

She cried quite shamelessly all the way back to school—secure in the fact that no one could see her.

In the sleigh the girls were beginning to recover.

"Jemima!" Betty said, breaking a long silence. "Poll saved all our lives; do you know it!"

Connie shivered. "I'm just beginning to realize it," she said, solemnly. "All the time everything was happening I was trying to remember the last duet I learned." Everybody laughed.

"Polly is—" Miss Crosby began. "Well, she's so splendid that— But I guess we'd better not talk about it. We're all on the verge of tears."

"Let's cheer for her," some one suggested. "Maybe we'll get our courage back."

They gave it—a long, long one—that had in it all their admiration and gratitude. And every poor tired muscle in Polly's valiant little body throbbed with joy at the sound.

CHAPTER IX

A STARTLING DISCOVERY

The next morning Polly stayed in bed for breakfast, as befitted a heroine, and received visitors. All the faculty came in, one after the other, to congratulate her. Miss Crosby's ability as a story-teller had served to picture the events of the night before in vivid colors, and Polly's splendid courage had not lost in the telling.

Lois and Betty kept watch at the door, and admitted only the girls that they knew Polly would want to see. They were not many, for she had a headache and was thoroughly tired. When the bell rang for study hour, they left Connie with her.

"Sit down and make yourself comfy. Here's a pillow." Polly threw one of Lois' to the foot of the bed, and Connie stuffed it behind her back.

"It's perfectly silly, my lying in bed like this," Polly went on, yawning and stretching luxuriously, "but Mrs. Baird insisted."

"I should think so. You must be nearly dead." Connie looked at her, wondering.

"Honestly, Poll, you were wonderful. How did you think of that hill, and have sense enough to go up it?"

Polly buried her head in the pillows and groaned.

"Not you too, Connie?" she asked, tragically. "Do I have to explain again that I was brought up with horses and have driven all my life, and been in any number of runaways, so that I am not afraid of any horse that lives? There, now, I've told you, and if you mention last night again, I'll ask Miss King to pull you out of my room by the hair of your head."

"I won't, I won't, on my oath!" Connie promised, laughing. "I'll even contradict all these people who are calling you a brave heroine, if you say so."

"I wish you would," Polly said, crossly. "Heroine! how perfectly silly."

65

"Of course it is, now that I come to think of it. You didn't do anything so great," Connie teased, "just stopped a couple of wildly running horses, and saved fifteen girls from sudden death—and what's that? A mere nothing."

"Connie, I'll—" Polly threatened, sitting up in bed, but Connie pushed her back. "You'll behave like a good child and answer me some questions."

"Well, go ahead and ask them."

"First, what's wrong with Dot Mead? I heard her say to one of the girls: 'Polly's bravery is so awfully evident, that it almost looks like showing off,' and when Dorothy Lansing said: 'I think so, too,' I simply couldn't help laughing. It was so like the Dorothys."

"Who were they talking to?" Polly asked, indifferently.

Connie smiled at a sudden recollection.

"A girl named Eleanor Trent. She was furious. She told them they were jealous cats. Imagine!"

Polly smiled grimly. "Eleanor Trent is on my team; she naturally would resent it. Hasn't Ange told you about the fuss yesterday, with the Dorothys?"

"No; what happened!" Connie was interested immediately. She felt this was a personal matter of her class. For the minute, she completely forgot she was only a visitor.

Polly described the scene on the hill—

"Three cheers for Betty!" Connie laughed, heartily. "I can just imagine her rage. But what is the matter with this Fanny!" she asked.

"Nobody knows." Polly shook her head. "We hurt her feelings early in the year, and I don't think she's ever forgiven us. I'm sorry, too; she's a dandy girl, if she'd only forget the chip on her shoulder."

"Going with the Dorothys won't help," Connie said, slowly.

"I know, but what can we do? Warn her that too much association with our classmates will not improve her disposition?" Polly unthinkingly imitated Miss Hale's manner.

66

"The Spartan," Connie laughed. "You might take Fanny up yourselves," she suggested.

"We might," Polly said, thoughtfully; "oh, there's the bell!"

Study hour was over, and a minute later, Lois, Betty, and Angela came in. There was an air of mystery about them, and Betty said: "Then you'll attend to it, Lo?"

"No; Miss Crosby's going to. I've just come from the studio," Lois answered, as she walked over to her bureau.

"Attend to what?" Polly demanded.

"Nothing!" Angela assured her. "Lo and Betty are fussing over some art secret."

"Oh, well, what's the news?"

"News?" Betty said, wearily. "Why, haven't you heard? Last night a girl hero stopped two rearing, plunging—"

"Betty, if you say one word more," Polly protested feebly—she was laughing in spite of herself.

"Hello, what's this?" Lois had been straightening Polly's dresser and discovered a note beside the pin cushion. "It's for you, Poll." She tossed it on the bed. "Must have been here since last night."

Polly opened and read it.

"Oh, what next?" she groaned. "Listen to this: 'To the captain of the basket ball team,' she read, 'I wish to say that I resign from your team to-day. Signed, Fanny Gerard.'"

"Why, she's crazy," Betty said, with indignation.

"That's the dear Dorothys," Angela remarked, airily. They were all discussing the note at once, when a tap sounded on the door.

"Go see who it is, Lo. I don't want to see any one else this morning," Polly protested.

Lois went to the door. They heard Jane's excited voice in the corridor.

67

"Please let us see Polly," she asked. "We won't stay a second."

"And we won't talk about last night," Phylis' voice joined in. "We've something awfully important to tell her and you."

Lois looked inquiringly at Polly and the other girls.

"Oh, let them in," Polly said, good naturedly. "Hello, you two, what's the secret?" she greeted them.

They came over to the bed. They were very much embarrassed by the presence of the others.

"You're not awfully sick, are you, Polly?" Phylis asked, real distress in her voice.

"Bless your heart, no," Polly assured her. "I'm just being lazy; I'll be up for luncheon."

"Tell us the something important," Lois said, pulling Jane down beside her on the window box.

Jane looked at Angela and Connie.

"Oh, never mind them," Lois said, understanding her hesitation. "What is it?"

"Well," Jane began, desperately, "I've got to tell you first—that Phylis and I were not very nice—"

"We listened behind a door," Phylis confessed, calmly; "we just had to."

"We were in Eleanor Trent's room," Jane took up the story again. "You see, yesterday she borrowed my gym shoes, and I went down to her room to get them. Well, you know her room is next to Fanny Gerard's, and just as we were coming out, we heard some one crying—"

"Fanny doesn't like us much," Phylis went on, "but we stopped to listen, and we heard Dorothy Mead say:

"'Well, don't be a baby about it. Of course, if you want to have Polly boss you, you can, and Fanny—'"

"No, then Dorothy Lansing said, 'you'd only have to coast down the hill once, to show her you wouldn't let her,'" Jane interrupted.

"Fanny was crying and saying she wanted to go home, and that she wouldn't ever speak to anybody again. We left them, and— Well, we thought we'd better tell you." Phylis ended the tale and looked at Polly.

"Poor Fanny," Polly sighed, "she's not very happy. The Dorothys shouldn't talk that way, of course, but it's not very important. Thanks for telling me, though. Don't listen any more. Fanny wouldn't like it." She treated the whole thing so lightly that both the younger girls thought they had attached more importance to the affair than was necessary. After they left, however, Polly sprang out of bed.

"Something must be done," she declared. Betty ground her teeth. "Jemima! I'd like to give both those Dorothys a ticket to the Fiji Islands," she said angrily. "They're spoiling our class."

"What about Fanny!" Lois inquired. "She's the one; evidently she's miserable, and look at that note."

Polly got back into bed.

"Everybody get out!" she ordered. "And, Bet, go find Fanny and ask her to come here. I'm going to talk to her. She's got some foolish idea in her head about us, and I'm going to find out what it is."

"What about the Dorothys?" Angela inquired, lazily. "Don't tire yourself out, Poll, they're not worth it."

"Oh, the Dorothys don't matter. They'll come around in time if we're nice to them. Of course, my being a heroine for the present won't help any," Polly said, with a grimace.

The interview with Fanny straightened everything out. Polly's surmise had been correct. Fanny was harboring the idea that, because Polly and Lois and Betty did not keep any love letters, they must, of course, consider her vain and foolish for doing it.

"I just know you all don't like me," she said, mournfully.

"Oh, Fanny, how silly you are." Polly laughed at her. "We did like you, and still do; you're loads of fun; you play basket ball wonderfully. You've no idea what a chance you have to be popular," she said, earnestly. "If you only wouldn't think everybody was trying to hurt your feelings. We really want to be friends."

It was a new experience for Polly to plead for friendship, but she did it, sincerely, and Fanny gave in. Lois and Betty joined them and a lasting peace was proclaimed.

Maud arrived in the afternoon. Mrs. Banks came with her, but acting under Mrs. Baird's advice, she did not spend the night. Lois and Betty and Polly took charge of them both for the afternoon. They showed them the school and grounds and, after Mrs. Banks left, they introduced Maud to all the girls.

Maud met them with a calm indifference, and looked them over with appraising eyes. Those she liked, she talked to. The others she ignored. The three girls were completely baffled.

"What'll we do with her?" Betty demanded. "Does she always act like this?" They were in the Assembly Hall before dinner. "Do you see anybody you'd like to meet?" she asked Maud a few minutes later.

"No, I don't," came the answer, without hesitation.

Lois laughed right out.

"Maud, you're too funny for words. Tell us what do you think of Seddon Hall?"

Maud gazed at her steadily for a moment.

"Oh, I like it no end," she said, warmly. "Why?"

"Nothing," Polly hastened to say, "we just thought perhaps you didn't."

The bell rang for dinner.

"You go down with your table," Lois explained. "You can do what you like, after dinner. We have a lecture to-night but it doesn't begin until eight."

Little did any of them guess how literally Maud would take Lois' words.

After dinner the Seniors were detained by Mrs. Baird to meet the lecturer and see that the Assembly Hall was in order. This took up their time.

The lecture was already on its way when Polly suddenly nudged Lois: "Lo, Maud is not here," she said in an agonized whisper, "what'll we do?"

Lois looked carefully all over the hall. Maud was nowhere in sight. "She's probably in her room," she whispered back.

They sat in nervous silence. The lecturer paused in his discourse for a minute.

"If I had a buttonhook and a piece of string," he said, turning to Mrs. Baird, "I could demonstrate what I mean."

Polly jumped from her seat, caught Mrs. Baird's eye, before any one else, and, in obedience to her nod, left the room.

She hurried over the Bridge of Sighs, for she hoped to get the articles required, and discover Maud without being absent from Assembly Hall too long. The sound of splashing made her stop and listen half way down the corridor. Some one was apparently taking a bath in the faculty tubs. She thought for a minute, and remembered all the teachers were on the platform. A horrible fear entered her mind. A second later the bark of a dog, followed by a low growl, crystallized the fear to a dreadful certainty.

She pushed open the door. Maud, her sleeves rolled up to the elbows, was kneeling beside the tub scrubbing a little wiry-haired yellow puppy, who was protesting vigorously.

Polly looked for a full minute, then she closed the door, and hurried over to her room.

When she got back to her seat, Lois whispered:

"See anything of Maud?"

"She's giving a dog a bath in the faculty's corridor," Polly answered, struggling to keep back the laughter.

"Poll!" Lois' jaw dropped, "I don't believe it," she said.

Polly knew that all the teachers would go to the reception hall for coffee before going back to their rooms. So the minute the lecture was over she called Betty and Lois. "Come with me, quick," she said, hurriedly, and led them back to the faculty corridor. The splashing had stopped. She opened the door.

"Jemima! What under the sun—" Betty and Lois could hardly believe their eyes.

Maud was still on her knees, but the dog was out of the tub; he stood shivering on the blue mat, while she rubbed him vigorously with a towel. She was not at all surprised to see the girls.

"Isn't he an old dear?" she asked, casually. "I found him out by the stables to-night when I was taking a walk. He needed a scrub most awfully."

Polly started to explain, thought better of it, and turned to Betty. The events that followed were swift and purposeful.

Betty washed out the tub, while Lois mopped up the water that the dog had splashed on the floor.

Polly took the astonished Maud with one arm and the very wet puppy under the other and hurried them, by way of the kitchen, into the furnace room.

"You can't have him in your room, you know," she said by way of explanation. "We'll tie him up here for to-night, where he'll be warm, and I'll get him some milk. You go up to your room as fast as you can. The bell has rung and you're supposed to go to bed right away. Can you find your way?"

Maud's brows drew together in a puzzled frown, but she didn't protest.

"Yes, of course," she said, wonderingly. "Good night, pup; I'll see you in the morning."

"Better hurry," Polly warned. "Good night."

"Good night," Maud said, cheerfully, as she went upstairs.

Polly followed her after she had found some food for the dog.

Betty and Lois were already in her room. Betty was stifling roars of laughter in one of Lois' pillows, and Lois was dabbing at her eyes and babbling foolishly.

Polly, the second the door was closed, threw herself down on her bed and gave vent to all the pent up mirth within her.

Finally Betty sat up.

"Oh, Lordy!" she choked; "how rare, how perfectly, gloriously, joyously rare. Think of Maud scrubbing a yellow pup in the faculty's private bath, and the Spartan liable to come in any minute. What a treat? Oh, Maud! I welcome you."

CHAPTER X

A SURPRISE TO MANY

Much to the disgust of all the girls, four days of warm sunshine had melted the snow, spoiled the coasting and made rubbers a first consideration.

The roads were hidden under inches of slush, the gutters were miniature brooks, and the ground seemed to be completely covered by a thick coating of red, oozy mud.

Polly, an empty basket over one arm, was picking her way gingerly along the back road that led from the farm.

As she came in sight of the gym, Betty met her.

"Hello, where are you going?" she demanded.

"I'm not going, I'm coming," Polly answered.

"Where from?"

"The cottage. I've just been to see McDonald; he's back from the hospital, you know, and Mrs. Baird sent me over with some fruit for him."

"Is he better?"

"Yes, but I don't believe he'll ever do any driving again; he's pretty feeble."

"Good old McDonald! It won't seem right not having him around; he's been here ever since I can remember, and that's six long years."

Betty gave a sigh to express great age, and resumed: "Do you remember the night you and he, between you, turned off the power for the lantern and got us out of a lecture by the Spartan's cousin?"

Polly chuckled. "McDonald was just talking about it. He said: 'Sure an' Miss Polly, I couldn't be after spoiling your evening, that I couldn't; so when I got back to the power house, I just let well enough alone, and all the time all I needed to do was to turn on the switch again.' I told him about Maud and the dog, and he laughed till he cried. What's doing this afternoon?"

"Nothing, absolutely nothing," Betty said dolefully. "The coasting's spoiled, and the gym is packed with girls."

"Then, that's where I'm going," Polly announced, "and you've got to come with me. Do you realize that February is not so very far away, and that our sub team is very, very weak?"

"I do," Betty answered, solemnly. "What are you going to do about it?"

"Find out who else can play. Bet, I can't lose either big game this year. We've just got to build up the team." Polly was very serious. "I'm worried."

"Who about?"

"Eleanor Trent; she can't get used to girls' rules, and she makes fouls all the time."

"Who subs for her?"

"Katherine Welbe, and she's no earthly good."

"Come on, then; let's see who's playing now," Betty gave in resignedly.

They went to the gym and sat down in the first row in the gallery. The game in progress was being played by Freshmen and Sophomores for the most part, and Jane and Phylis seemed to be doing most of it. They were both playing jumping centers. It was not very exciting to watch; some one fumbled or made a foul every other minute and the whistle sounded incessantly.

"I hoped Maud would be here," Polly said, thoughtfully. "Have you seen her to-day?"

"Yes, she's up watching Lois paint, I think. You know she draws awfully well herself. Did you see the pen and ink sketch she did of her little yellow pup, yesterday? It was great."

The question of the dog had been solved by Polly. She had received permission from Mrs. Baird—who had laughed heartily at the story—for Maud to go round to the stable and see him after school hours.

"Yes, she showed it to me," Polly answered Betty's question. "Then Lo made her let her show it to Miss Crosby. But that's not basket ball." She returned to the original subject abruptly. "I'll tell you what I'm going to do, as soon as this game is over. I'll ask Miss Stuart if we can't have the gym to ourselves for practice."

"Do you mean the big team?" Betty asked. She was not very anxious to change into her gym suit for so short a time.

"No; I'm going to pick out some of these girls and find Maud and make her come. Then I'm going to change them around in different positions. I'll bet I'll find some one that's good at something."

"Well, what do you want me to do?" Betty stood up ready to act. "Go find Maud?"

"Darling Betty, if you would be so kind," Polly teased. "I'll be — what is it Maud says? — 'no end grateful'; then come back and help me."

Miss Stuart not only granted Polly the permission she asked, but stopped the game at once. "It will give you more time," she said, "and I'm not sorry to give up my whistle to you."

When Betty returned with Maud they began.

"I met Fanny on my way over, and I told her you wanted her. I thought she might as well help, too," Betty said.

"Good! she can watch the guards. You watch the centers and I'll take the forwards. Maud, I'm going to put you on as a guard; you're so tall."

"Oh, all right," Maud agreed, "what do I do?"

"You keep the ball away from the girls of the other team. Wait till we start, then I'll show you." Polly, a minute later, blew the whistle and placed the teams. Jane and Phylis were so excited that they nearly forgot to jump when she threw the ball up between them.

For two hours and a half they worked. Polly and Betty and Fanny explaining and showing them how, and now and again getting into the game themselves.

While they were struggling with clumsy forwards and slow guards, Lois, who really ought to have been there, was having a very important talk with Mrs. Baird and Miss Crosby.

"Do you think Polly knows anything about it?" Mrs. Baird asked. "I do hope not."

"She hasn't the slightest idea," Lois assured her. "Betty just told me she would be in the gym all afternoon, so there's no chance of her seeing any of the preparations."

"Hadn't you better fix the table?" Miss Crosby asked. "Here's everything for it, I think; do the rest of the girls understand?"

"I spoke to Miss Lane about the younger children eating at the Senior table," Mrs. Baird said. "The girls all know I've told each one." Lois was gathering up yards of pale green crepe paper as she spoke. "I think it will be a lot of fun, don't you? And Polly will be awfully surprised."

The mystery of this conversation was not explained until dinner time that night.

Polly and Betty came in, hot and tired from playing and just in time to take a shower and dress before study hour. It is true that Polly might have noticed that some of the girls were exchanging mysterious glances behind their desks, had it not been for the fact that a letter from Bob claimed her attention. She found it on her desk.

"Dear Polly," she read.

"Hark to the joyful news. My foot is all well, and I've started training. I haven't forgotten what you said, and every time I think I'm no good I just say: Cheer up, May's a long way off. Wish me luck.

"Bob."

Polly was so delighted that she spent the rest of study hour trying to compose a fitting answer, and she was so anxious to tell Lois on the way to dinner that she didn't realize she was being led into the lower school's dining-room, until she was at the very door.

"Where are we going?" she asked, turning suddenly.

"Come and see; we're having dinner in here this evening," Lois answered, as she opened the door and displayed a table decorated with green paper with a centerpiece of pale pink roses.

Mrs. Baird was standing at one end, and Miss Crosby at the other. The rest of the places were filled by the girls who had been on the eventful straw-ride.

Lois led Polly, too surprised to speak, to her place at Mrs. Baird's right, and there she found a big box tied with green ribbon with her name on it. Every one was looking at it, and Polly realized in a dreamy sort of way that she was expected to open it. All she could say was:

"Why, er, what—" she was so astonished.

She opened the box and discovered a bulky chamois bag packed in with tissue paper. She looked at it, wondering, and then gave an exclamation of joy, when she discovered that it covered a big silver loving cup. On one side was engraved the date and the words: "To Polly, in grateful recollection of her splendid courage," and on the other, the names of all the girls, Connie's included, who had been on the ride.

Polly looked at it for a long time, without a word. Then she turned, appealingly, to Mrs. Baird.

"What can I say?" she asked. "I can't think of anything but 'thank you.' And that's so little. Though if I could only be sure you knew how much I meant by it, it would be enough. Do say you know," she pleaded, looking around the table, "because I'm terribly embarrassed," she ended, laughing.

"Very good speech, Poll," Betty teased from her seat opposite, "and quite long enough; my soup's cold."

"Betty!" Mrs. Baird tried to look shocked, and failed, because she simply had to smile.

Then followed the happiest meal imaginable. At the end a big cake, with Polly's name on it, was brought in, and then everybody told her all over again how brave she'd been.

"But I wasn't," she insisted. "It was just a simple thing to do—nothing that really took courage."

"You may be right," Betty told her, "but you'll never find any one to agree with you."

Polly smiled. "If I do," she said, "will you promise never to mention it to me again?"

"Yes," Betty said, promptly; "I will."

"All right."

After dinner she led the way, followed by all fifteen girls, straight to Maud. They found her in one of the class rooms.

"Tell her just what I did," Polly directed.

And Betty described the ride in her most extravagant style. Finally she displayed the cup.

"Now, what do you think of it?" she ended triumphantly.

Maud's eyes had been wide with interest throughout the recital. She looked at Polly with perfect understanding.

"By Jove!" she said earnestly, "wasn't it lucky the hill was there. Did you remember to rub the horses down when you got back, Polly?"

There was a second's silence.

"Yes, and I put blankets on them," Polly answered. Then, turning to Betty: "Do I win?" she asked, laughing.

CHAPTER XI
THE CONCERT

"'Flow gently sweet Afton among thy green braes,'" caroled Betty. She was picking out the accompaniment with her first finger on the Assembly Hall piano, one stormy afternoon, for the benefit of Angela and Polly. They were trying to compose a Senior class song to Seddon Hall.

"'Flow gently, I'll sing thee a song in thy praise.'"

"That ought to do," she said, abruptly swinging around on the piano stool to face them.

"The rhythm is good and I love the tune."

Polly and Angela considered for a moment.

"It is rather nice," Polly agreed, "if we can only find words to fit it."

"That's easy, use the same idea as the song," Betty suggested. "Supplement Hudson for Afton, and—"

"Oh, Bet, how can you?" Angela's poetic taste objected. "Imagine a school song that began 'Flow gently sweet Hudson.' I suppose you'd go on with: 'Among thy sign bordered banks.' It would never do, would it, Polly?"

Polly was laughing too hard to reply at once.

"I don't know; it would be original, anyway, Ange," she said at last.

"And you know our class has always been original," Betty reminded her.

"There's a difference between originality and silly nonsense, but I suppose it's too much to expect either of you to appreciate it," Angela said, with dignity.

Betty played a loud chord on the piano.

"Ange, when you're crushing, I always feel like running away," she said, timidly. "However, I still protest that there's nothing wrong with telling the Hudson to flow gently," she added. "Of course, I'm open to argument."

Angela was exasperated. The rest of the Senior class had appointed these three to write the class song, over a week ago. It had to be ready before the Senior concert. This was as far as they had gotten.

Christmas vacation began the next week, and the concert was to be the night before. Angela felt, that given a piece of paper, a pencil and a quiet place, she could compose a fitting song, but with Betty and Polly saying ridiculous things every minute to make her laugh, she couldn't think of even one sensible line.

"You can't use the words, gently and sweet, in relation to a mighty river like the Hudson." She referred to Betty's question. "You might as well call it a cute little brook," she finished in disgust.

"Why, Angela! I do believe you're cross." Polly looked up in sudden surprise at the irritable note in Angela's voice. "What's the matter?"

"Nothing but a cold in my head and pages of Virgil translations," Angela replied, woefully. "You and Betty won't be serious for a minute. It'll mean I have to sit up the night before the concert with a wet towel around my head and write a song that won't be any good."

"Polly, we ought to be ashamed. Angela's right," Betty said with sudden seriousness. "From this minute on, I promise to behave," she added solemnly, "and agree to anything you say. We'll discard 'Flow gently sweet Hudson,' as no good, and proceed."

"How about starting 'On Majestic Hudson's Banks?'" suggested Polly.

"We can't use majestic, it's too long and grand's a horrid word." Angela considered, frowning.

"Well, leave out the adjective and say:

"On Hudson's bank

Stands fair Seddon Hall —

"That's all right, listen, I'll play it."

They sang the words to Betty's accompaniment.

"Truth, honor and joy

Is her message to all."

Angela added inspired:

"Her daughters are loyal" —

Betty would have gone on, but Polly stopped her.

"I won't agree to that, every class song I ever heard, said exactly the same thing," she protested. "Let's get something about happiness."

"Hardly more original." Betty laughed, but Angela interrupted.

"I know what Poll means. How's this?"

"There's no limit to" —

"Slang," Polly said abruptly.

"It isn't really."

"Yes, it is. 'Common usage often converts the most ordinary phrase into slang or colloquialism. The writer should take care to avoid them,'" Betty quoted. "Try limitless depth."

"All right, that's better still," Angela agreed.

"There's a limitless depth

To her bounteous store."

"Oh, marvelous!" Polly exclaimed. "What rhymes with store — paw, law, door, war, more — More, that's it."

"Each year she gives of — her — her — We can't use bounty again. Give me a word somebody."

"Riches," Betty suggested.

"Of her riches the more.

"Oh, that's perfect!"

Angela didn't exactly agree, but she didn't say so. Instead she gave them the verse she had just composed.

"Each daughter has shared

In the wealth of her days,

United we join now

In singing her praise."

"Jemima, one of us has a brilliant mind!" Betty exclaimed. "That's too good to forget. Wait till I find a pencil."

There was one in the pocket of her sailor suit and she wrote the words down on the back of a sheet of music.

"Why, that's three verses," she said as she finished with a flourish.

"Let's add one more!" Polly suggested, "with Seddon Hall in it and something about leaving like this:

"And when the time comes" —

"Yes, I know," Betty interrupted eagerly.

"When we must depart" —

"That's good, but I like each, better than we," Polly said critically.

"And when the time comes

When each must depart"

"Finish it for us, Ange."

"The memory of Seddon Hall

Will remain in our hearts."

Angela chanted promptly. "Seddon Hall is rather too long for the line but I guess it will do."

"Of course it will!" Polly assured her, as Betty scribbled hurriedly. "We'll claim poetic license. I'm sure it's worth it. Let's go find the girls, and read it to them."

"Where are they?" Angela inquired. "I think the Dorothys have gone to the village."

"Evelin's in the gym, and Mildred's in the Infirmary," Betty said. "Where's Lo?"

"In the studio." Polly closed the lid of the piano, preparatory to leaving.

"Well, we can get her at any rate," Betty said. "Come on."

Fanny was in the studio with Lois, when they got there. Ever since Polly's promise of friendship, she had been with one or the other of the three girls. Even Angela had taken an interest in her, now and then.

As the friendship grew, and the girls found that she "filled the want that the year lacked," as Betty put it drolly:

"Fanny's so nice and such a relief just because she isn't 'us.'" By this she probably meant that the little Southerner would always see things differently from the three who, though totally different, thought and looked at things in pretty much the same way.

"We've finished the song," Polly announced, proudly, as they entered the studio.

Lois looked up from her drawing board.

"I've nearly finished the poster. How do you like it?"

The girls crowded around her, to admire a crayon sketch of a group of wakes dressed in costume, singing. There was a house like Ann Hathaway's cottage in the background, and a big yellow moon just rising behind a hill.

They were delighted with it.

"Just right, Lo!" Polly insisted. "It ought to be English because all the ballads we're going to sing are early English—'Good King Wenceslas Looked Out' and 'God rest ye, Merry Gentlemen,'—and the rest."

"Oh! I adore those old things," Fanny said eagerly. "We always sing them down home, every year."

"Read the song," Lois demanded. "I'm crazy to hear it."

"Hadn't I better go?" Fanny offered. "I'm not a Senior."

"Oh, never mind," Polly said, "you won't tell."

"Just the same, I'll go. Will you all have tea in my room this afternoon? I've just gotten a box of cookies from down home," she asked at the door.

"We will," Betty replied without hesitation. "Tea and homemade cookies are the one thing I need after my labors."

The others accepted with equal enthusiasm and Fanny left to prepare for them.

When she had gone, Betty seated herself on the window seat and referred to the piece of music.

"Here's the song entire," she announced. "We all helped with, but most of it is Angela's."

"I knew that," Lois said with a grin, but Betty ignored the interruption.

"The tune is 'Flow gently Sweet Afton' and the song is dedicated to Seddon Hall, with apologies to Robert Burns. Here it is," and she read:

"On Hudson's bank
  Stands fair Seddon Hall.
Truth, honor and joy
  Is her message to all."

"That's the first verse."

"Go on," Lois prompted, "I like it."

"Each daughter has shared
  In the wealth of her days.
United, we join
  In singing her praise.
"There's a limitless depth
  To her bounteous store,
And yearly she gives
  Of her riches the more.

"And when the time comes
  When each must depart,
The memory of Seddon Hall
  Will remain in our heart."

"Somehow it sounds better when it's sung," Betty said, wonderingly. The poem was not quite up to her expectations, but Lois' enthusiasm banished all doubts.

"I think it's great, and I know the others will too. Isn't it a relief to have it finished? All my poster needs now is the printing, and Maud's promised to do it for me in Old English Script."

"Fine, but put your things away, and let's go over to Fannie's room. Those cakes call." Betty smacked her lips in anticipation as she helped Lois collect her materials.

Fanny was singing as they entered Junior Mansions. It was an old Negro melody, and the crooning notes were soft and beautiful.

"Why I didn't know Fanny could sing," Polly exclaimed in surprise, and the rest stopped to listen.

"'Swing low, sweet chariot— I'se comin' for to carry you home'"—

The music ended abruptly, and they heard the rattle of the cups.

"Why didn't you ever tell us you had a beautiful voice?" demanded Betty between cookies, a few minutes later. "You ought to be studying."

"The very idea!" Fanny laughed in reply.

"Hasn't anybody ever told you you had before?" Lois asked wonderingly. But Fanny shook her head.

"I reckon they none of them ever had time to pay any attention to me," she said. "They were always busy listening to my cousin."

"Which cousin?" Polly inquired.

"Caroline," Fanny said. "We were brought up together, and when we were little, Mammy Jones used to say: 'Honey, the only way for to do, if you wants to sing, is to swaller a hummin' bird.' One day Caroline came in and said 'she had swallowed one.' Well, later, she did develop a lovely voice you know, and poor mammy believed till the day she died that 'Miss Carrie had done swallered a hummin' bird.'" The girls were delighted.

"How rare," Betty chuckled.

"Bless her old heart," Polly added. "Where's Caroline now?"

"In Washington. She's studying both voice and piano."

"I don't believe her voice is any sweeter than yours," Lois insisted. Fanny shook her head.

"Maybe not, but everybody thinks so, so there you are. Carrie just naturally does get ahead of me in everything. I told you she cut me out with one of my beaux," she added, laughing at herself. "A thing she could never have done two months before."

Three days later the discovery of Fannie's voice proved of much more importance than any of the girls had foreseen. Evelin Hatfield, who had a very clear soprano voice, and who had been cast for the solo parts in the concert, came down with tonsilitis and had to go to the Infirmary. The Seniors met in English room to discuss finding a substitute, after Miss King had assured them that there was no chance of Evelin's immediate recovery.

"Of course it's a Senior concert, and as long as I can remember no one has ever helped them out, but our class is hopeless," Lois said. "Evelin's was the only real voice, except yours, Ange, and you're already cast for the King. Do you think you could take the page's part in 'Good King Wenceslas,' Dot?" she asked Dorothy Lansing.

"Goodness! No! Why, I'd be scared to death," she answered hastily.

"Then there's nothing to do, but to ask one of the Juniors to help us," Polly said decidedly. "She could leave the platform when we sang our song."

The rest agreed. "But who?" Helen inquired.

"Fanny Gerard has a sweet voice, and I know she knows the carols," Betty said, "and she's a Junior."

There was a little discussion before Fanny was selected, but in the end Betty carried her point.

The few days before the musical were taken up with rehearsals. The party was to be very informal—just something to do on the last night. The Seniors sang carols in costumes and later on served light refreshments.

Fanny was delighted to sing. The day of the concert she went out with Polly and Lois to get evergreen branches to decorate the hall with, and between them they turned the platform into a veritable forest.

By seven-thirty the school was assembled, and at a quarter to eight the Seniors entered. They marched around the room and up to the platform singing: "God rest ye, Merry Gentlemen." Fanny's clear voice was so above the others that the girls and teachers began to whisper among themselves. There was a lull of expectancy as they began "Good King Wenceslas looked out on the feast of Stephan."

Angela, who was dressed as the King, sang her part:

"Haste thee, page, and stand by me,

If thou knowest it telling,

Yonder peasant, who is he?

Where, and what, his dwelling?"

With so much expression that the deficiency of her voice was overlooked.

But it was Fanny, in her green page suit that was to score the triumph of the evening. She stepped out a little from the others, when her turn came to answer the King.

"Sire, he lives a good league hence—

Underneath the mountain.

Right beyond the forest fence

By Saint Agnes' fountain."

Her notes were full and beautiful, and the sympathetic quality of her voice enchanted her audience. They broke out into enthusiastic applause.

"I told you so," Betty whispered as Fanny bowed her thanks.

The rest of the evening may be truly said to have belonged to Fanny. Even the Seniors' class song was hurriedly applauded, so that she might return to the platform.

The girls made her sit down at the piano when the carols were over, and sing them song after song.

At nine o'clock, Betty insisted that she stop long enough to have some refreshments.

"You all don't really think I can sing, do you?" she asked seriously, when they had joined Polly and Lois and Angela.

"Of course we do," everybody told her with enthusiasm.

"You've swallowed a bird all right," Betty laughed.

Fanny shook her head. So much praise was embarrassing.

"Maybe I did," she said shyly, "but it was probably nothing but a poor no account sparrow."

CHAPTER XII

CHRISTMAS

The two-seated sleigh jingled merrily up the drive and stopped at the carriage block. Polly and Lois jumped out and turned to help Mrs. Farwell.

"Home again," Polly exclaimed, joyfully looking around her with pardonable pride, for the splendid old house they were about to enter was her own, and every corner of it held the dearest of memories.

Lois and her mother were no less delighted to return to it. It had been Uncle Roddy's suggestion that they all spend Christmas there, and every one had heartily agreed to it.

"How splendid it looks in the snow, doesn't it?" Mrs. Farwell asked. "My, I shall be glad to see an open fire-place. I hope Sarah has started a fire in the drawing-room. Just put the bags in the hall, Tim," she added, to the old coachman who was busy unloading the back of the sleigh. He nodded respectfully.

"Where's Sandy?" Polly demanded, "I thought he'd be here to meet me, surely."

Tim shook his head. "He's gettin' old, Miss Polly," he said. "And he spends most of his time lying before the fire."

Sandy was Polly's beautiful big collie. She found him as Tim had said, a few minutes later, after Sarah had opened the door for them and ushered them in with a hearty welcome. He was lying on the hearth rug in the library. And as he heard Polly tip-toe in, he got up stiffly and held out his paw.

"Darling old fellow," Polly said, dropping to her knees beside him, and patting his silky head.

Sandy licked her hand affectionately and made as great a fuss about her, as his rheumatic old joints would permit. Then Lois claimed her and together they roamed over the house, enjoying the spacious rooms and reveling in the blazing wood fires.

Bob and Jim arrived the next day with Dr. Farwell and Uncle Roddy. The sleigh was not large enough for Polly and Lois to go and meet them. So, to make up for it, Bob and Polly hitched Banker, the pony, to the cutter, later in the afternoon, and drove out into the woods in search of a Christmas tree.

"Get a nice bushy one," Lois called after them, as they drove off. "And don't get lost."

Bob tucked the rug around Polly's feet. "We won't," he called back. "Which direction?" he inquired.

"Down the hill and take the first turn to the right," Polly told him. "Jemima! but it's cold." And she snuggled down in her furs. "I can't believe this is Christmas Eve."

"Neither can I," Bob said. "What's this I hear about you and Lois going to visit some one for New Year's?"

"We're going to Fanny Gerard's," Polly answered. "Won't it be fun? She lives in South Carolina. We're going specially for her New Year's dance. It's the event of the season—and I'm so excited. I was afraid when the letter came, Aunt Kate wouldn't let us go—their being strangers—and it's so far, but it seems your darling father knew all about old Mr. Gerard and his sister, so it was all right, and we leave December thirtieth—taking with us our very best clothes," she added, smiling.

There was something like disapproval in Bob's patient silence.

"Well, I hope you have a good time," he said, finally. "But what you want to leave this place for to go South is more than I can see. It's just like girls. They'd cross the country to dance. I think it's a crazy idea, if you ask me," he added with vehemence.

"But I didn't, Bobby," Polly answered sweetly. "Oh, there's a wonderful tree! It's just the right size and it's bushy," she exclaimed suddenly. "Do let's get it."

Bob pulled Banker in, and fumbled under the seat for the ax. But when they got out Polly found she had lost sight of the tree and they had to wade around in the snow up to their knees for fully ten minutes before they found another that suited them. They cut it down, dragged it to the sleigh and bore it home in triumph. It was dark long before they reached the house, and they found everybody dressed for dinner and waiting for them in the library.

"Oh, we've had a glorious ride!" Polly said brightly. Her cheeks were whipped red from the wind and her eyes sparkled.

"Is the tree bushy enough for you, Lo?" Bob asked.

"Yes, it's a beauty," Lois said, examining it.

"You two should have been with us," Polly said, speaking to Jim, "just to have seen Bobby work."

"While Polly told me how to do it," Bob said, teasingly. "You'd think, to hear her talk, she'd cut down trees all her life. When she found that I wasn't paying any attention to her, she got back in the sleigh and recited 'Woodman Spare That Tree' from the depths of the nice warm robes while I froze."

"Bob," said Polly, indignantly, "if you'll let me pass, I'd like to go upstairs and dress for dinner."

That evening, they decorated the tree, that is, Lois and Jim did most of it while Polly and Bob rested in two big chairs before the fire, with Sandy between them, and made suggestions.

"Jim, that tinsel would look much better going around the tree instead of up and down," Bob said critically.

Jim, who was upon a stepladder, went on trimming, while Lois came to his defense.

"Bob, do you know what tinsel is supposed to represent," she asked.

"Isn't supposed to represent anything," Bob said calmly.

Lois looked at Jim in sympathetic understanding. "You see, he doesn't know," she said. "Tinsel, dear brother, is supposed to represent the silver rays of the stars," she explained.

"Oh, get out," Bob objected. "It's no such thing. Anyway, that has nothing to do with putting it around the tree."

"Robert, you grieve me." Jim shook his head mournfully. "You a college man. How could the rays of the stars go around a tree? I ask it in all seriousness."

Bob was fairly caught. Even Polly laughed at him. Mrs. Farwell came in just in time to save him from more teasing.

"Oh, how beautiful the tree looks," she said. "I wouldn't put another thing on it, it's quite perfect as it is. Come into the other room and sing some carols, and then we must all hang up our stockings and go to bed; to-morrow will be a busy day."

"What are we going to do besides eat dinner?" Uncle Roddy demanded from the other room.

"Why, Sarah is packing some baskets for Polly to take to some of the poor families in the village," Mrs. Farwell explained, "and of course, we'll all go to church in the morning. In the afternoon I suppose—"

"Now, Kate," interrupted the Doctor, laughing, "In the afternoon do let us digest our dinner."

After they had all sung the carols around the old tinkly piano, they wished one another a Merry Christmas, found their candles on the big table in the hall—for there were no electric lights in Polly's house—and went upstairs.

"Come along old man," Polly said to Sandy. "Do you want some help?" she asked, as the old dog prepared to follow her. He always slept on the rug beside her bed.

"How feeble he is," Bob said. "He doesn't act a bit well, Poll."

"It's old age, I'm afraid," Polly replied, sadly. "He's over fourteen, you know."

"I'm going to carry him up," Bob said. "I believe it hurts him to take these steps." He picked up Sandy ever so gently and carried him to Polly's room. "Good night again," he said at the door, "and Merry Christmas."

But all the wishes in the world cannot make happiness. That Christmas Day was far from merry for either Polly or Bob.

About two o'clock in the morning Polly awoke with a start. Some one was groaning. As she sat up in bed and tried to rub the sleep from her eyes, she felt something touch her arm. It was Sandy's paw.

After groping about in the dark she found the matches and lighted her candle, and jumped out on the floor.

"What is it, boy?" she asked, resting his head in her lap.

Sandy rolled his eyes, as dogs do when they are in pain and the agonized appeal in them made a lump rise in Polly's throat.

"Dear old fellow, what is it?" she said, gently. "What can I do for you!" She was seized with sudden fright. It seemed as if she alone was awake in all that black, still night. She called Lois two or three times but got no reply. She went to the door and listened. Her friend's regular breathing came to her faintly from the other room.

"What can I do?" she whispered. "Oh, Sandy boy, don't," she pleaded as the dog groaned again.

A minute later, she was hurrying into her clothes. When she was dressed she tip-toed down the hall and knocked at the farthest door. "Bob," she called softly.

"Yes," came the instant reply. "What is it?" Fortunately the wind had rattled his shade, so that the noise had awakened him a few minutes before.

"Get up," Polly called. "Sandy's awfully sick and I'm frightened."

Bob hurried into his things with full speed and joined her. Together they carried the dog into the morning room at the head of the stairs, and put him on the lounge. Bob lit the lamp.

"He can't breathe," Polly said desperately. "Oh, Bob, what can we do?"

Bob went for water and moistened the dog's tongue while Polly held his head in her arms. His breathing grew more labored.

"Could Tim do anything?" Bob suggested, forlornly. He knew that he couldn't, but it was terrible to just watch the dog suffer.

Polly shook her head. She didn't dare trust herself to speak. After a little while the breathing grew quieter. Sandy turned his head and licked Polly's hand. Then quite suddenly it stopped — his body trembled and he lay still in her arms.

Bob put his hand on her shoulder.

"Better leave him, Poll," he said huskily.

Polly looked up at him. It was a second before she understood.

"Bob, he's not— Oh, Sandy! You've left me," she sobbed, and buried her head in his silky coat.

All Christmas day Polly tried to keep up her spirits and not spoil the others' pleasure, but her heart had a dull, lonely ache that wouldn't go away. Any one who has loved and lost a faithful dog understands. And Polly had loved Sandy from his first puppy days.

All the family did their best to cheer her up, but the day was a woeful failure. Uncle Roddy and Bob were the only ones who understood her grief, and their own was so great that they could find no words of comfort.

After dinner she disappeared. She knew that all the afternoon callers would be dropping in to exchange greetings, and she could not bear the thought of talking to them.

Bob found her about four o'clock, curled up on her favorite window seat, at the head of the stairs. He had been despatched by his mother to tell her that some of her friends were in the drawing-room.

"If she doesn't want to come don't urge her," she had warned him. "I'll make some excuse."

"Bobby, I just can't," Polly said when he had told her. "My eyes are all swollen and I've such a headache."

"What you need is air," Bob said decidedly. "Go get your coat and hat, and we'll fly off with Banker for a little ride. Come on, Poll," he coaxed, "it will do you loads of good."

Polly gave in reluctantly.

"Where are we going?" she asked when they were in the sleigh.

"Never mind, I've a scheme," Bob told her. "Shut your eyes." He headed the pony toward the bay. The cold air acted as a tonic on Polly. By the time they stopped before an old tumble down fisherman's hut, she was quite herself again.

"Why, it's Uncle Cy's place!" she exclaimed. "Bobby, how did you ever think of him?"

They pushed open the door, without knocking, and entered the one little room that served for all purposes.

Uncle Cy was one of Polly's earliest and best of friends; he was an old fisherman. They had spent many long, happy days together, when she was a little girl. He welcomed her heartily.

"Why, Miss Polly. I was beginning to think I'd have to go one Christmas without a word from you," he said. "How are you? You're getting mighty handsome," he teased "and I'm sorry to see it. I never did hold with handsome women. 'Handsome is as handsome does,' I always say," he added with a wink. "And you, Mr. Bob, how do you do again? That basket you brought me this morning was mighty good," he said with a chuckle.

"We're just here for a second," Polly explained. "Banker's freezing outside. Have you had a Merry Christmas?" she asked brightly. No one could be unhappy long under the spell of Uncle Cy's genial smile.

"Fair to middling," the old man answered, contentedly. "Have a seat," he offered.

They stayed chatting for a few minutes more, and then returned to the sleigh.

"The old darling," Polly laughed, "he hasn't changed a bit."

When they reached home, they stole in the back way. One of Lois' merry laughs greeted them as they entered.

"Jimmy, you wretch," they heard her cry.

"What's the matter, Lo?" Bob inquired from the door of the drawing-room.

Lois looked up in confusion.

"Jim kissed me under the mistletoe," she said, "after I'd expressly told him not to."

Polly joined in the laugh that followed.

"Bobby," she said as they were taking off their coats in the hall, "I'm ashamed of being such a baby to-day. I acted as if I were eight years old."

Bob pulled a big wadded handkerchief out of one of his pockets. "Don't apologize, Poll," he said. "Look at this. I wasn't so very grown up myself." Then he added, gently, "Good old Sandy."

CHAPTER XIII

POLLY'S LETTER

Polly and Lois left for Fanny's the following Thursday and arrived the day before the dance. A description of their good time can best be gotten by reading Polly's letter to Betty, which was written a few days after:

"Dearest Betty:

"What a shame you couldn't be here. I know it's mean to tell you, but you've really missed the funniest kind of a time.

"I do hope your mother is much better by now. Please give her both Lois' and my love.

"And now to tell you all about the dance — as I promised. So many things happened it's hard to know where to begin. The first day I guess —

"Well, we arrived at this adorable little town about ten o'clock in the morning, and I thought when I looked out of our window as the train pulled in, that I was dreaming and it was a story book village. The sun was shining and it was as warm as toast. I don't know why the fact that the grass was green made such an impression on me, but it did. We've had so much snow up home that I couldn't believe there could be summer anywhere else.

"Is this lengthy description boring you, Betty dear? What is it Miss Porter always says, 'Create your atmosphere first, before you begin your story.' That's what I'm doing and you'll just have to be patient while I create a little longer. I simply must tell you about the funny little cabins. They're all over the place. A relic from the days of slavery, I suppose, and they're so little — just a room or two — that you gasp when you see large families standing out in front of them. It's beyond me to figure out how they can all go to sleep at once.

"Lois suggests that they take turns and I think she must be right. The little pickaninnies are too sweet for words; they have innumerable little braids sticking out all over their heads, and their big black eyes just dance with impishness. You'd love them.

"Fanny lives in a most wonderful story book house. It's red brick that's really pink. Oh, you know what I mean! And it's trimmed with white. Big colonial pillars up the front, and a lot of little balconies jut out where you least expect them. I have one out of my window, and every night I play Juliet to an imaginary Romeo in the rose garden below. Lo insists I am getting sentimental, but it's only the effect of the 'Sunny South,' which brings me, no matter how indirectly, to the boys we've met—and the dance!

"Oh, Bet, such a lark! There were over a hundred people—both old and young, and even then the ballroom—oh, yes, the Gerards have a ballroom—looked half empty. We danced from ten o'clock until four in the morning, and went for a picnic the next day. Imagine!

"Fanny looked beautiful. She wore a lovely white dress without a touch of color on it, and it just set off her wonderful dark hair to perfection. The cousin, Caroline Gerard, is here at the house, too. You know, the one Fanny said could sing, and who 'just naturally gets ahead of her.' Well! Intermission of four minutes.

"No use, I've been struggling with my better self, but I can't resist the temptation to tell you just what Lo and I think of her. Betty, she's horrid. I mean it! She's so conceited and sure of herself and without the least reason to be. She looks a lot like Fanny, but with a difference. She's larger and much more definite, if you know what I mean, and she walks into a room with a 'Well, here I come' sort of an air. She completely puts Fanny in the background. I'll tell you later, how Lo and I pulled her out again—Fanny I mean—but now, I'll go back to the dance.

"Caroline was there of course. She wore a wonderful red gown and carried a big yellow ostrich fan. She looked like a Spanish dancer. It took me all evening to get used to her. The combination was rather startling. Lo, in spite of her dislike, wanted to paint her. I did not—jealousy, on my part of course—for every time she came near me, she killed my lovely green frock. You see, before I came down stairs, I looked in the glass and I rather fancied that I looked quite nice, but, I turned pale by comparison, and naturally I didn't like it. Are you getting curious about Lois? I hope so, I'm saving her on purpose for the end. Betty, she was the belle of the ball. You can't, no, not even with your imagination, picture her. She looked like some lovely fairy. But you know that dreamy style of hers. Well, just try and see her in your mind — draped in yards and yards of pale yellow chiffon, with touches of blue here and there, — and you'll understand the effect. Her gown was just nothing but graceful soft folds. I tell you everybody went quite mad about her, and you know how beautifully she dances. — Excuse me, that's the luncheon gong — I'll finish later.

"Ten P.M.

"Hello, again Bet:

"It's late and I'm oh, so sleepy, but I must go on. Let's see where was I? Oh, yes, clothes. But poor dear you must feel as if you'd been reading a fashion book, so I'll skip the rest of the dresses, which really didn't amount to anything, and go on with the dance.

"Of course we met so many people that I can't even remember their names, but some of my dances stand out rather vividly in my mind. Do you know, Southern boys can say more pretty things in one minute than our boys up North can in a whole month. Don't think I consider it a virtue, far from it. I think they're awfully silly — on top. Of course underneath they're splendid — just like boys anywhere else — but certainly they are more fun to talk to.

"I danced the first dance with Fanny's 'Jack.' He's quite as handsome as she said and he came to the dance in his uniform. After the music had stopped we went out in the rose garden for a walk.

"Betty, what can a girl say, when a boy tells her she is fit company for roses and moonlight? If there is a proper answer, I certainly couldn't think of it at the time and I did the very last thing I should have done — I laughed — and I went on laughing as he waxed more eloquent. Finally I said:

"'Oh, for pity's sake, do stop and talk sense.' He looked as if he had never heard the word.

"'You're very hard to please,' he said in oh, such offended tones. 'What shall we talk about?'

100

"'Why not Fanny,' I suggested; 'she's the only subject we have in common, except flowers and birds and moonlight, and we seem to have exhausted those.'

"'But I'm very fond of Fanny!' he said quite feelingly. I told him I was too and that we ought to make the best of it. I explained how popular she was at school, and how she'd made the team, and raved at great length over her voice. And do you know what that boy did? When I stopped for breath he stood stock still in the middle of the path and looked at me, then he whistled.

"'Well, I'll be darned.' It was the first natural thing I'd heard him say. 'I never met a girl before in all my life that would talk that way about even her best friend,' he said.

"The music started then, and we had to hurry back—but, Bet, what do you suppose he meant?

"Lois evidently had much the same trouble understanding her partners. I heard her say—'how absurd' during supper, and it sounded so like you that I was startled for a second.

"Oh dear, I almost forgot to tell you the funniest thing that happened through the whole evening. Poor Fanny, being hostess, had to dance with all the clumsy, unattractive boys that were there, and every time I saw her, she seemed to be having a dreadful time of it. I think it was the eighth dance and I was sitting out with a boy named Wilfred Grey—the one Caroline cut Fanny out with, you remember? I was arguing with him about clothes—he said he preferred bright colors, and I insisted there was nothing as lovely as white. Of course we both knew he really meant Caroline, and Fanny. Well anyway, in the middle of the dance—we were in a sort of a little alcove—Fanny came by pulling a big, lanky youth after her. I never saw anything so funny; he was just walking, and making no kind of an effort to keep to the music. Mr. Grey and I laughed about it, and when they came around again, we were watching for them. Imagine our joy when they stopped just beside us, and we heard Fanny say, in that killing way of hers:

"'Look here, Sam Ramsby, if you'll get on my feet and stay there, I'll tote you around this room, but this jumping on and off is more than I can stand.' Betty, wasn't that rare — it was the best minute of the whole evening. Lo is furious that she missed it.

"Mercy! It's twelve o'clock and I must go to bed. Lo is going to add a P.S. to-morrow. Please appreciate this long letter as I've really spent much valuable time over it.

"Sleepily,

"POLLY."

Lois' postscript followed.

"Hello, Bet:

"I've just read Polly's scrawl, and I must really smile. If Caroline's dress made hers look pale you may believe it was at long range, for I never saw Poll the entire evening that she wasn't completely surrounded and hidden from view by a flock of dress suits. Wait until you see the green dress and you'll understand why.

"Polly says she promised to tell you about Fanny's triumph and forgot to. Personally, I'm glad she left me something easy. I know it will amuse you. It happened the first night we got here. There were a lot of Fanny's friends at dinner and in the evening we played games and Caroline sang. Poll has described her, but not her voice. It's one of those big throaty ones that quaver, and she sings the most dramatic of love songs. I hated it, it was so affected. Well of course, everybody raved about it and complimented her and asked for more. They didn't really want it, but Caroline has a way of insisting upon the center of the stage.

"She didn't stop until everybody was thoroughly tired of her and of music generally. Then Polly surprised every one by saying quite calmly: 'Fanny I wish you'd sing for us now.' Caroline couldn't understand. 'Why, Fanny can't sing,' she said. I don't think she meant to, but it was out before she could stop it. I was cross.

"'Oh, yes, she can,' I told her, 'the girls at school are crazy about her voice. Sing that pretty French song Fanny.' Poll joined in and we teased so hard that she finally did sing.

"Bet, I do wish you could have seen those people, they were overcome with astonishment. They were so used to Caroline talking of nothing but her voice that they had never thought of Fanny. But after that first song, I thought they would never let her stop. There, that's the story. Caroline hasn't been asked to sing since and Polly and I are mean enough to be just as pleased as punch. I must stop this instant. We'll see you next week at good old Seddon Hall. In the meantime, loads of love. I won't be sorry to get back. How about you?

"Affectionately,

"LOIS."

CHAPTER XIV
MAUD'S DISAPPEARANCE

There was no need to consult the calendar. The subdued voices, and the worried frowns, to be seen in any of the corridors or classrooms of Seddon Hall proclaimed it the first of February, and examination week. Every girl carried a book under her arm and the phrase, "Do you think you passed?" was on every one's lips.

Outside the weather was clear and cold, the pond was frozen smooth as glass. The snow on the hill was packed solid and fit for coasting, but no one ventured that far away from their books.

The first half of the year was over and the girls knew from past experience that the rest of the time would hurry by. In one short month there would be a hint of spring in the air, and commencement would be in sight.

On this particular afternoon the Senior class were having their examination in Latin and, to judge by their frowns, they were finding it difficult.

Betty ruffled her hair every little while and scowled at Miss Hale, who was correcting papers at her desk. She had answered all the questions she could and done all the prose work. All that was left was a translation of Virgil. Betty stared at the unfamiliar text, and wondered where it had come from. "I don't believe it's Virgil," she said to herself. "If it is it's a part we haven't had." Then a few words from the confusing paragraphs caught her eye, and she began to remember. Her brow cleared—a few words were all Betty ever needed to start her on one of her famous translations. She wrote hurriedly for ten minutes.

"That will do, I guess. The Spartan's sure to say, 'a little too free, but correct on the whole,' anyway," she thought, ruefully, as she folded up her paper and put her pen and ink away.

Miss Hale raised her eyebrows in surprise as she handed in the examination.

"You have finished very early," she said, coldly, and Betty's heart sank. "Don't you want to look over your paper?"

"Jemima, no!" Betty exclaimed, without thinking. "That is, I beg your pardon, Miss Hale, but I don't think I do. You see I'd begin to wonder about all my answers and that would only make things worse," she said, desperately.

"Very well; you may leave the room," Miss Hale replied, with a resigned sigh that plunged Betty into the deepest gloom.

She wandered over to Senior Alley. It was deserted. The rest of her classmates were still in the study hall. She found Angela's history book on her bed and started to study, but gave it up in despair. They had covered over half of a thick book that year and there was no way of knowing what part to re-study.

"I'd be sure to learn all the dates that weren't asked for," she said, aloud, and closed the book.

She thought of the possible Juniors who might be free. She had passed Fanny on her way out of the study hall—she remembered the big ink spot that she had on one cheek. Suddenly she thought of Maud.

"I'll bet she's finished her exam, if she had one," she laughed to herself, for Maud's utter disregard of lessons that did not interest her was a much-discussed topic.

She went upstairs to the Sophomore corridor, expecting to find it almost as deserted as her own, but, instead, she found five of the teachers talking excitedly in the hall.

Mrs. Baird had her hand on the knob of Maud's door. Betty was a little confused at such a strange gathering.

"Excuse me," she said, hastily, and turned to go.

There was no need to explain that something was wrong—the whole atmosphere of the corridor was charged with mystery.

"Don't go, Betty," Mrs. Baird said, peremptorily, "I have something to tell you; perhaps you can help. Have you seen Maud to-day?"

Betty shook her head. "No," she said, slowly, "I don't think I have."

Mrs. Baird hesitated for a minute and then said, very distinctly:

"Maud is lost."

It was a startling announcement, and Betty couldn't understand. Who ever heard of any one being lost at Seddon Hall.

"But how?" she asked Mrs. Baird. "Where could she be?" Miss Crosby answered her:

"Nobody knows, Betty," she said. "Maud was at breakfast this morning, but at luncheon time she did not appear. I sent one of the girls up to look for her and she came back and told me she couldn't find her. I thought perhaps she was in the Infirmary, but after luncheon I asked Miss King, and she said she hadn't seen her."

"She's not in the building; we've looked everywhere," Mrs. Baird continued. "Where could she have gone? None of the teachers gave her permission to go out of bounds."

At the word permission Betty looked up. It struck her that Maud might not have considered it necessary to ask for permission.

"May I go to her room?" she asked Mrs. Baird.

"Certainly."

Betty opened the door and looked up at the wall over the bed. As she had expected Maud's snow shoes were gone from their accustomed place. She explained to the teachers.

"She's probably miles away by now," she finished. "Did she have any examination this afternoon?"

"Yes, in literature," Miss Porter told her, "and I can't believe she'd cut—"

"She wouldn't—not literature anyway," Betty said, confidently, and turned to Mrs. Baird.

"I'm sure I can find her by tracing her snow shoes," she said.

"But you mustn't go alone; something may have happened. Take one of the stable boys with you," Mrs. Baird answered.

"I'd rather have Polly and Lois," Betty said, "if there's anything wrong."

"Very well, where are they?" Mrs. Baird asked.

"Taking their Latin exams," Betty told her.

"Go and get them. I'll explain to Miss Hale, and, Betty, dear, do make haste; I'm really worried; the child may have hurt herself somewhere."

Betty hurried to the study hall. She knew it was useless to try to explain to Miss Hale; so she said: "Mrs. Baird wanted Polly and Lois at once." They handed in their papers and joined her in the corridor. She hurried them to their room, and explained on the way.

Fifteen minutes later they had found the track of Maud's snow shoes and started out to follow it.

Seddon Hall owned over five hundred acres of land and for the most part it was dense woodland. Trailing through it in winter without snow shoes was hard work, for the snow drifted even with the high boulders in places and you were apt to suddenly wade in up to your waist. Maud had taken the path that went out towards flat rock. This made following her tracks comparatively easy for the girls.

"What under the sun do you suppose has happened to her?" Polly demanded.

"I don't know," Betty replied; "I wish I knew when she'd started. As far as I can find out no one has seen her since breakfast."

"Did she have an exam this morning?" Lois inquired.

"No; her class had Latin and she doesn't take it. I'm not awfully worried," Polly said, suddenly. "I would be if it were any one but Maud. She's used to much wilder country than this and I can't help feeling that she's all right somewhere."

"But, where?" Lois demanded. "If she were all right and hadn't hurt herself she'd have been home by now."

"If she's kept up on top of the hill she can't have come to very great grief," Betty declared, "but if she's headed down to the river — then, anything could have happened."

"What do you mean?" Lois asked.

"Why, she might have fallen and broken her leg," Betty explained. "You know how dangerous those rocks are in winter; she may have stepped between two of them and gotten caught."

"Don't," Lois protested, with a shudder.

They trudged on for a quarter of a mile in silence, then the trail turned suddenly to the right.

"She's gone toward the apple orchard, thank goodness!" Betty exclaimed.

"Do you suppose she's gone round by way of the bridge and home?" Lois asked, stopping. "If she has, we'll have our hunt in vain."

Polly and Betty considered a minute. Then Polly said:

"Of course not; if she had, she'd have been home hours ago."

When they reached the apple orchard they noticed that the print of the snow shoes was less regular.

"She's stopped to rest here," Betty said, pointing to the ground. "Look how irregular these prints are."

"Come on!" Polly said, quickening her steps, "we may be near her."

"Hold on!" Betty cried, "look, something happened here; it looks as if she'd fallen down!" A big dent in the snow, as if a body had been lying on the ground, showed up in the prints of Maud's snow shoes.

"Here's a queer thing," Lois pointed out, "one shoe's going in one direction and one in another."

Polly walked on a little way, and then called to the others, excitedly:

"Here are the prints and look, side of them there's a mark as if she were dragging something along with her."

"What's that black spot farther on?" Lois demanded.

They looked in the direction in which she pointed and saw, a couple of hundred yards farther on, something that showed black against the snow.

"It's a man's hat! Oh, Poll, I'm scared to death," Lois said, trembling, when they came up to it. Murder and every possible form of highway robbery passed through her mind.

Betty turned white, and Polly bit her lip.

"Come on!" she said, bravely, "we've got to find her."

"Jemima!" Betty groaned; "it's beginning to snow, too." She picked up the hat; it was almost buried by the snow, and looked green with age. They were tired by this time—walking in snow shoes is very much easier than trudging in rubber boots—and they realized with a shudder that Maud and her unknown companion had a long start of them.

They followed the track as fast as they could. It went on through the orchard and down the hill, and then over the bridge. It stopped there and zigzagged in every direction. The girls looked and exchanged frightened glances. Betty's heart was beating furiously and Lois' knees trembled. They forged on, the prints were clear again, and went straight up the hill, always accompanied by the queer, uneven path beside them.

"She must be dragging something," Polly said. "That's all that that track can mean."

"Or some one is dragging her," Lois spoke the thought that was uppermost in Betty's mind.

"Nonsense!" Polly ejaculated. "I don't believe it. I tell you Maud is all right, wherever she is. I know it."

The road they were taking was a short cut to school. There was a steep hill—a level stretch, and then it joined the road from the school farm. The snow was falling heavily, and it was getting dark when they reached the top of the hill, and the prints were fast disappearing. By the time they got to the road they lost all track.

"Whatever happened, Maud's home," Betty exclaimed in a relieved voice, and broke into a run. The others followed her.

Mrs. Baird was walking up and down the Senior porch as they came up.

"Oh, girls! I'm so glad you're back; come in and take off those wet clothes right away; Maud's here."

"Is she all right?" they asked in chorus.

"Yes," Mrs. Baird assured them. "She must have been in the building when you started out."

"Where?" Betty demanded.

"In the bath-tub," Mrs. Baird said, hurriedly. "I'll explain it to you later. Now do go and change; you must be very wet. I'll have some hot soup for you in my sitting-room. Come as soon as you can. I'll excuse you from study hour."

The girls hurried upstairs without a word. In Senior Alley they met Fanny.

"Do you know where Maud Banks is?" Betty asked her.

"Yes; she's in her room," Fanny said; "where have you all—"

"Go up and tell her to come down here this minute," Betty interrupted her; "please, Fanny, like a dear," she added as an afterthought.

Fanny went up to the corridor and returned with Maud.

Polly and Lois and Betty were all changing their clothes in their separate rooms. Maud stood in the hall between, with the astonished Fanny.

"Did you get lost?" Betty asked the first question.

"No, rather not," Maud answered; "got out as far as an apple orchard, and it was awfully late. I'd no idea where the time went. I knew there must be a short cut, so I—"

"Never mind, we know that," Polly interrupted. "Did you sit down in the orchard?"

"As a matter of fact, I did; my snow shoe was loose. How did you know?"

"Were you dragging anything when you left the orchard?" Lois demanded.

"Yes, a branch of a tree; I say, I'm awfully sorry you had all that trouble of—"

"Did you see a man's hat by any chance, on your way to the bridge?" Betty asked.

"Yes." Maud was becoming more and more bewildered.

"What did you do when you got home?"

"Why, I hustled down to Roman Alley and took a tub. You see I was awfully late, and I knew that Miss—what's her name—Spartan would be no end cross if I didn't show up for the exam. I didn't want to miss it either; it was literature, you know."

"Where did you leave your snow shoes?"

"Up against the gym porch; they were awfully wet and I didn't want to take the time to go to my room. I say it was a bit of a joke; you're thinking I was lost, wasn't it?" she asked, calmly.

Polly finished buttoning her dress.

"Maud," she said sternly "go back upstairs. To-morrow we may be able to see the joke, but not now."

Maud left with Fanny. "I'm most awfully sorry," were her last words.

A few minutes later, the girls sought the comfort of Mrs. Baird's charming sitting-room, and the promised hot soup.

Between sips they told her the story of their hunt and the fears that beset them. She listened delightedly, but with ready sympathy.

"You poor, dear children! What an experience! I talked to Maud very severely."

Betty thought she said: "I will talk."

"Don't tell her what we've told you," she begged, "I wouldn't have her know for anything."

"She'd say it was no end of a joke," Polly laughed.

Mrs. Baird nodded in understanding.

"Of course I won't tell her," she said merrily. "It's a secret just between us," she added with a smile.

CHAPTER XV

THE JUNIOR PROM

Polly and Lois were busily packing their suitcases, while Betty and Angela stood by and offered suggestions. They were leaving on the afternoon train for Cambridge to attend the Junior Prom. Bob and Jim had finally prevailed upon Mrs. Farwell to let them come. Barring the party at Fanny's this was their first big dance, and they were both frankly excited about it.

"What time does your mother get here?" Betty asked. "Is she coming up to school?"

"No; we're going to meet her at the Junction, where we change for the Boston train," Lois replied.

"Oh, I'm sorry; I hoped I was going to see her." Betty was very fond of Mrs. Farwell.

"She'll be here for Commencement," Polly said, "so will Uncle Roddy; he's crazy to see you again. And this summer we're going to have a big house party, Ange. You've got to come this time with Bet."

"I'd love it, if you won't insist on my breaking in colts, and— Look out, Lo! if you don't wrap up those slippers in tissue paper they'll be all scratched—"

"I haven't any tissue paper; won't a towel do?"

"Yes; here, I'll throw you one."

"Mercy! I almost forgot my silk stockings," Polly exclaimed. "Get them out of my bottom drawer for me, will you, Bet, like an angel?"

Betty hunted in the drawer. "They're not here."

"Then look on the closet shelf."

"Here they are. Mercy, aren't they beauties! butterflies embroidered on them!" Betty drew one on over her hand and admired it.

"That's Lo's taste," Polly said. "She gave them to me for Christmas. There, I think that's everything." She surveyed her neatly packed bag. "I do hope my dress won't be wrinkled."

"What are you going to wear for an evening coat?" Angela inquired.

"Our capes," Lois answered.

"You'll freeze to death, and the hoods will crush your hair."

"Well, what will we do?" Lois asked. "Wear veils?"

Angela considered a minute, and then left the room to return with a long scarf of maline over her arm.

"Here, take this, one of you; wait till we decide which one it's the more becoming to." She put it around Polly's neck and drew part of it up over her hair.

"Very sweet, but," Betty said, "try it on, Lo."

"Perfect! you get it," she said, as they viewed the effect, and certainly the soft, flimsy tulle did make a charming background for Lois' delicate beauty.

"Polly, you need something more severe," Angela said.

"I've a wonderful Roman scarf; it's all lovely pale shades. I'll get it; wait a shake," Betty offered. "There you are," she said, triumphantly, when she had pulled it tightly around Polly's head. "You look Italian; all you need is a pitcher on your shoulder."

"It might interfere with my dancing," Polly laughed. "Thanks, ever so much, Betty dear; I'll lend you my butterfly stockings when you go up to West Point."

"Then, don't you dare dance holes in them," Betty warned. "Perhaps you'd better not dance at all; it might be safer," she added.

"Just find a nice comfortable chair and sit in it and keep your feet off the floor," Angela suggested. "Then, if any one asks you to dance, why, tell them that you'd like to but Betty says you mustn't."

"I've taken enough clothes for a month." Lois looked despairingly at her bag. "Sit on it, will you, Bet?" Together they closed it and Lois locked it as a precaution against its flying open.

"It's nearly time to start." Polly consulted her watch. "I'm so excited my heart's in my mouth."

"There's your carriage; it's waiting," Angela said, looking out of the window. "You'd better hurry. Here, I'll take one bag." Betty took the other, while Polly and Lois tried frantically to pull on their gloves.

"Be sure and remember everything," Betty said, as they ran downstairs, "so you can tell me how to act next week."

"We will," Polly promised.

They met Mrs. Farwell an hour later and took the train for Boston.

"I had a letter from Bob this morning," she told them. "He says that he will not be able to see us until luncheon time to-morrow; he's awfully busy, I suppose."

"Maybe he's trying to find partners for us," Lois laughed, "and he's not finding it easy."

Polly groaned: "Oh, Aunt Kate," she said, "suppose we have to sit out half the dances."

Mrs. Farwell laughed.

"I wouldn't worry about it, if I were you," she said, confidently; "you can trust Bob to see to that."

The next day, Jim and Bob joined them at luncheon, at one o'clock.

"Why didn't you meet us yesterday?" Lois demanded when they were seated at the table.

"Couldn't do it," Bob told her.

"But we're at your service this afternoon," Jim added. "What do you want to do?"

"Why don't you just sit and talk, up in our sitting-room," Mrs. Farwell suggested. "If you do anything else the girls will be tired out for the dance."

114

"What, and waste all the beautiful afternoon? Oh, mother!" Bob objected. "Besides," he added, winking at Jim, "if we sit and talk, as you suggest, the girls will be tired. You know Lois?"

"Oh, Bobby, aren't you mean?" Lois said. "I don't talk nearly as much as you do."

"How about taking a ride in my car?" Jim suggested. "It's a warm day."

"Oh, Jim!" Mrs. Farwell said, "I'm afraid to let them."

"But you come, too," Jim urged. "We could all crowd in."

Mrs. Farwell shook her head.

"No; I must rest; my head really aches," she said.

"Then, let us go," Bob teased. "Just for a short ride. You'll hurt Jim's feelings if you don't; he's awfully proud of Pegasus."

"Pegasus? Is that the name of the car?" Mrs. Farwell laughed. "Well—" she hesitated.

"We'll promise not to go one bit faster than thirty miles an hour," Jim assured her.

"And I'll blow the horn all the way, mother darling," Lois added. "I hope it's a nice, noisy Claxon? Is it, Jim?"

"Better than that," he told her, "it has three notes, and you can play a tune on it."

"May we go, Aunt Kate?" Polly asked, anxiously. "We really will be careful."

Mrs. Farwell looked from one to the other.

"Yes," she said, slowly, "but you must be back by four o'clock."

"Oh, mother; make it five," Bob teased.

"No; four o'clock." Mrs. Farwell was determined. "The girls must rest."

Jim left to get his car. In less than half an hour they heard his horn blow.

"He's here; hurry up," Bob said. "Don't make him stop the engine."

Mrs. Farwell pulled the girls' furs up close about their necks and went down to see them off.

"Now, do be careful," she said, earnestly. "Remember, Jim, no fast driving."

"Not even if I see a fine road ahead with no cars in sight," he promised her solemnly.

"And that means a whole lot for Jim," Bob explained. "He's rather proud of his driving, mother, and it's an awful disappointment to him when he can't show off."

"Nonsense; I don't believe it," she called after them; "I know he'll be careful."

The car, or "Pegasus," to give it its proper title, was long and gray and shaped like a boat. It was really a roadster, but a small seat opened up in the back to accommodate two people.

Bob and Polly climbed into it, and Lois took her place beside Jim. They drove slowly through the city.

"Where to?" Jim inquired.

"Anywhere," Lois said, "as long as we go. Isn't this air wonderful? Why, it's like spring."

Jim headed the car in the direction of Salem and the speedometer registered thirty miles.

"Why didn't you promise mother not to go over forty miles an hour?" Lois asked.

"Because I knew she wouldn't let us go," Jim replied. "Isn't this fast enough for you?"

Lois looked up at him over her brown furs.

"Do you know," she said, slowly, "my one ambition is to go sixty miles an hour in a car."

Jim gasped for a second. He was tempted, but he said: "Sorry I can't take you."

"Of course you can't to-day," Lois agreed. "But will you some time?"

"You bet," Jim promised, enthusiastically. "Bob's asked me to visit him this summer, you know," he added; "maybe we can try it then. Would you like to drive?" he asked when they were well out of the city.

"I don't know how," Lois said, sorrowfully.

"Well, I'll teach you." Jim stopped the car.

"What's the matter?' Bob called.

"Nothing," Jim said, "I'm going to let Lois drive; that's all."

"Oh, Jim, have pity on us!" Polly begged; "we do want to go to the dance to-night."

"Don't worry," he answered, "you'll get there."

"Now," he said to Lois, when they had changed places, "push that back; it's the brake, and you want to release it. There, now put your foot on that; that feeds gas in the engine. No, do it gently," he said, as the car jerked forward.

Lois' face was set in firm determination, and she obeyed instructions without a word. After she had stalled the car several times, and Bob had gotten out to crank it, she finally started.

A motor van coming towards them made her almost run into a ditch. But Jim took the wheel in time.

"You know, you don't have to climb trees and fences, Lo," Bob teased; "there's really plenty of room on the road."

"Oh, but it looked as if it would run right into us!" she exclaimed, shuddering. "Suppose it had taken off one of our wheels?"

"Keep still, Bob," Jim directed. "Don't talk to the chauffeur."

They drove on for a few miles more and were beginning to consider turning, when the car began to miss and make terrifying noises.

"What's it doing?" Lois demanded. "Have I broken it?"

Jim laughed heartily. "No," he said, "change places with me. I'll fix it."

But Pegasus refused to be fixed. It went on a little farther, and then stopped.

Jim and Bob got out. They opened the hood. "Nothing wrong here," Jim said. "I wonder what's up!"

"I'll spin it," Bob suggested. They worked for nearly fifteen minutes, but the car would not budge.

"I know I did something to it," Lois turned tearfully to Polly; "now we'll never get home."

"Oh, yes we will; we can get some one to pull us, I guess," Polly comforted her. "Maybe there's no more gasoline," she said to Bob.

The boys looked at each other and then burst out laughing. Jim investigated the tank and then took off his hat and bowed respectfully to Polly.

"You are quite right; there is no gas, and I'm a — well — I'm a very brilliant driver. Will you please tell me how you ever thought of it?"

Polly laughed. "Why, that's what always happens to Uncle Roddy's car when he goes out," she said. "He never remembers the gas. Sometimes he pulls the poor car to pieces before he thinks of it."

Jim felt comforted.

"Well, I guess I'll go see what I can do about getting some. Bob, you stay here with the girls."

"Somebody has to call up Aunt Kate," Polly reminded them, "we won't be home by four, and she'll be worried."

"Then Bob's got to do it," Jim said, decidedly. "I'll never be able to face her after all my promises."

"All right!" Bob said. "I see a house down the road."

"Perhaps they'll have some gas," Jim said, hopefully, as they started off.

But it was after seven before they finally got back to the hotel. Jim had had to walk miles before he could get a pail of gasoline, and then on the way back one of the tires had blown out.

Mrs. Farwell was waiting for them in the lobby. She looked thoroughly frightened.

"Children, where have you been?" she asked.

Bob explained.

"We couldn't get here a second sooner," he concluded.

"I'm awfully sorry, Mrs. Farwell," Jim added, apologetically, "I never felt so ashamed in my life; but I really did start with plenty of gas, only the tank leaked," he finished ruefully.

Mrs. Farwell smiled her forgiveness.

"You'll have to hurry through dinner, then go and dress," she said. "Perhaps, after all, the girls aren't so very tired."

Polly put her arm around her.

"Tired?" she said, happily, "why, Aunt Kate, I feel as if I could dance all night."

"So do I, mother darling," Lois insisted.

"Well, that's very probably just what you will do," Mrs. Farwell answered with a resigned sigh.

Bob and Jim, after a very hasty dinner, hurried to their rooms to change their clothes, and were back before either of the girls were ready, for Mrs. Farwell had insisted upon an hour's rest. When they did join the boys, they were looking their best. They had on the same yellow and green dresses that they had worn at Fanny's party.

Bob and Jim were secretly delighted. There is always a good-natured rivalry at a Junior Prom and they both felt that the girls' charming appearance gave them a decided advantage over the other men.

When they arrived at the Union the dance had already started, and the floor was crowded with people. Lois and Polly were so carried away by excitement that the whole evening passed in a whirl of delight.

Mrs. Farwell had been right the day before when she had promised her that Bob would see that they had plenty of partners, for Jim and he brought up all their friends and introduced them.

As Polly said afterward, in answer to Betty's questions.

"There were so many of them that I couldn't begin to remember their names. I just called them all Mr. Er—"

"What was the hall like?" Betty had demanded of Lois.

"Mercy! I don't remember," she said, "except that it had two big fireplaces and the most fascinating chandeliers made of deers' antlers."

Betty had been disgusted at this hazy description.

It was after two o'clock before they got back to the hotel, and they were both so sleepy that they could hardly thank Bob and Jim for their good time.

As the boys went back to their rooms, Jim said: "Bob, do you think the girls will ever forgive me for this afternoon?"

"Why, of course," Bob assured him. "They didn't mind being late. Polly would rather motor than dance any day."

"H'm!" Jim replied, slowly, "but it happens to be Lois that I'm worrying about."

"Well, you needn't," Bob answered, laughing. "When I was dancing with her to-night, I asked her if she didn't like you better than she used to, and she said: 'Oh, lots, Bobby; I think he's a duck.'"

CHAPTER XVI

MUMPS

"Cheer up, Polly! it can't be as bad as all that," Betty said, laughing, in spite of herself. For the spectacle of her friend's woe-begone expression was too exaggerated to be funny.

"I didn't think the game was so bad," Lois remarked, cheerfully; "nothing to worry over."

They had just returned from the gym, where the regular team had been practicing in preparation for the coming indoor meet.

February was almost at an end, and the girls had completely recovered from the Junior Prom. The date for the game was settled, and Seddon Hall was to play the Whitehead school team the following week.

"If we were only playing in our own gym," Polly said, forlornly, "we might have a chance; but to have to travel for an hour on the train first, have luncheon in a new place, and then play in a strange gym, why we'll none of us be up to our best."

"You talk as if we were all very nervous and highly strung children," Betty said, impatiently. "We've all played in other gyms before."

"Fanny never has," Lois reminded her.

"Well, what of it? She won't get scared. I know her better than you do," Betty insisted. "We've two more days to practice, anyway."

"Two more days? Do you suppose that's enough time for Eleanor to learn not to make fouls, and for Fanny to learn your passes?" Polly demanded. "It's all very well for you to be cheerful; you're not captain."

"But worrying won't help any, Poll," Lois said, quietly. "If you are going to get in a blue funk, what can you expect of the others?"

"Nothing!" Polly answered; "I know I'm silly, but that team beat us last year on our own floor, and our team was twice as strong then as it is now."

Lois and Betty gave up arguing. They understood exactly how Polly felt, but they knew, too, as soon as the game began she could be depended upon to regain her courage and hope.

The next two days the team worked hard. They practiced passes and signals, and Eleanor did her best to remember the unaccustomed lines. By Saturday morning Polly felt a little more cheerful.

"What time do we leave?" Lois asked, after breakfast. "Ten-thirty?"

"Yes; and I'm going to post a notice that every one is to be ready at ten. Then I'll be sure of them," Polly said.

"I wish we could take Maud as a sub, instead of Caroline Webb," Lois said, slowly. "She's worth more."

Polly shook her head. "It doesn't matter, really," she said. "Our sub-team is so weak that we simply can't rely on it. We'll have to play it all through ourselves, and we mustn't get hurt; that's all there is to it. If one of us gets out of this game to-day, it will mean we lose," she concluded, decidedly.

"Oh, captain, how do you feel?" Betty inquired, coming in with her gym suit over her arm. "I've been talking to some of the girls; they're just sufficiently nervous — all except Eleanor — she's too cocksure. I don't like it," she added, shaking her head doubtfully. No one knew better than she how dangerous over-confidence was before a game; it was much more liable to prove disastrous than a severe case of fear.

"I'll talk to her," Polly said. "Don't worry; she'll get over any extra amount of confidence when she sees the other team — that is, if they're the size they were last year."

"Which I hope and pray they are not," Lois added, fervently.

They started at ten-thirty, after a little delay caused by Fanny forgetting her gym shoes, and Betty her favorite hair ribbon. The school gave them a hearty send-off, cheering the carryall as far as the gate.

They arrived at Whitehead in time for luncheon.

"They don't seem awfully cheerful here," Polly said, when she and Lois were alone for a minute. "I wonder what's the matter?"

"Doris Bates, you know, the girl who plays forward, told me she had a terrible sore throat," Lois replied. "Perhaps she's given it to the rest."

"I have an idea they'll use their subs," Polly said. "If they do—" She let Lois finish the remainder of the sentence for herself.

The game began at two o'clock. The Whitehead gymnasium was a big, high ceilinged room with small windows. It was really a converted barn. The light was so poor that on winter afternoons they had always to use the big arc lamps that were incased in wire, and hung at either end of the room. There was no gallery for the spectators. They sat around in groups wherever they could find a place. Some of them were so near the lines that Polly felt sure she would run into them and, hardest drawback of all, the floor was slippery. The school used the gym for all their entertainments and it had been waxed not a week before.

Polly took in all these disadvantages at once and realized their probable effect on her team.

"Don't lose your nerve or your head," she said, cautioning them before the game started. "The lights are a bother, but try not to pay any attention to them. If you hit them, never mind. Be careful of the floor, and if you want to go after a ball, let the girls on the side lines look out for you."

"I do wish they'd move back," Fanny said, almost tearfully. "They might just as well be following you around, holding your hand? They're so close I declare I can hear them breathing."

"The lines are awfully faint," Eleanor said, dejectedly. She was looking hard at the big broad-shouldered girl it would be her duty to guard.

Polly glanced from one face to the other. Even Lois' and Betty's reflected apprehension. She sighed.

"Remember," she said, as they took their places, "we're playing for Seddon Hall."

When the first whistle blew she felt that she was facing a sure defeat and she tried valiantly to keep her glance from straying in the direction of the silver cup. But, as the game progressed, she discovered that, though her team was heavily handicapped, the only danger that they really had to face was surprise. For they had expected to fight, and fight hard for every point, and they were totally unprepared for the unexplainable collapse of the opposing team. From the very start, the ball was theirs. It took time for them to recover from the shock before they could use their advantage. Before the end of the first half, Whitehead had put in four substitutes.

"What can be the matter?" Lois demanded between halves. "Why, they're not putting up any fight at all."

"They're all sick," Betty said. "Both the centers have terrible colds. It's a shame."

The second half was a repetition of the first, and Seddon Hall won an easy victory.

Polly felt that she had not really earned the cup when it was presented to her at the close of the game.

The score was twenty-seven to nothing in their favor.

"It's too bad your team are all laid up," she said to the other captain. "I'm sorry; I know that we would never have made such a score if you'd all been well."

The other girl smiled. "Why you won it fairly," she said. "We played a miserable game. A few colds shouldn't have made all that difference. I don't know what happened to us."

"Well, you'll have a chance for revenge next year," Polly answered with a parting nod.

The return of the team lacked something of its triumphal spirit. There is never the same feeling of exhilaration over an easily won struggle that there is over a hard fought one. And though the rest of the girls welcomed the return of the cup, there was a general feeling of sympathy for the other team, rather than enthusiastic praise for their own.

Polly and Betty were still puzzling over the whole thing two days later in the study hall, when Lois joined them and solved the mystery.

"I have an awful sore throat. What do you suppose is the matter with me? I don't feel like doing a thing," she said.

"Better go and see Miss King," Polly advised. "You look sort of tired and sick."

"I think I will," Lois said.

In the Infirmary a few minutes later, Miss King looked down her throat and prodded the outside. "How long have you felt this way?" she asked.

"Only yesterday and to-day," Lois told her. "Don't say I have to go to bed, please."

"Sorry," Miss King said, briskly, "but you do. Don't go downstairs again; go right in here; I'll get your things."

"What have I got?" Lois demanded.

The nurse shook her head. "Nothing much, I hope," she said, "but I want you to go to bed."

Next morning Lois awoke in the Infirmary to see Miss King standing at the foot of the bed.

"What are you laughing at?" she asked, sleepily.

Miss King gave her a hand glass before replying.

Lois sat up in bed and looked at herself. Both sides of her face were swollen.

"Mumps!" she exclaimed. "Oh, what a sight I am," she added, laughing.

Polly and Betty came up to inquire for her, after breakfast, and heard the news.

"Mumps!" they both said at once. And Polly cried. "Why, Betty, that's what was wrong with the Whitehead team."

"Of course, sore throats and everything. I'll bet they all came down with it the next day," Betty exclaimed. "No wonder they couldn't play any kind of a game."

Lois did not remain alone in the Infirmary for long. One by one the team joined her. Polly was the first. During study hour that night her throat began to hurt. She felt it; it was suspiciously lumpy.

"Here I am," she said the next morning, when Miss King had pronounced it mumps.

"Oh, Poll!" Lois was delighted. "You look funnier than I do. Only one side is swelling and it makes you look top heavy."

Polly surveyed herself in the mirror.

"That's easily fixed," she said. "Watch!"

She undid her hair and rolled it into a round knob under one ear. "There, now it's even."

"But it doesn't match," Lois objected. "You look like a pie-bald pony now."

Polly glanced about the room. A round celluloid powder-box caught her eye. She emptied the powder out and fitted the box over her hair.

"That better?" she inquired.

Lois was still laughing over this absurd picture, when the door opened, and in walked Betty and Fanny.

"You two?" Polly exclaimed. "Oh, what a lark!"

"When did you get it?" Lois asked.

"Suddenly, last night, at dinner," Betty answered. "We had salad with French dressing. And, oh, when I swallowed that vinegar!"

"I certainly did think I was going to choke to death," Fanny said, feelingly. "I jumped right up from the table."

"Yes, and knocked over a glass of water," Betty prompted, "and announced to the whole dining-room that you reckoned you had the mumps. Everybody laughed so hard they couldn't eat any more dinner," she concluded.

"I'm so glad you both got it," Polly said.

"Do you suppose we'll look like you two do to-morrow?" Betty asked rudely.

"Worse, probably," Lois consoled her.

Eleanor and Evelin came down with it the next day. After that there were no more cases. Fortunately, it did not spread throughout the school. Perhaps some of the girls were disappointed, for the stories of the good time in the Infirmary made school seem very stupid by comparison.

One day Miss King brought Betty a note from Angela. It was wrapped around a copy of the Gossip, the Whitehead school paper.

"Dear Mumpy (she wrote):

"Read the news item on page ten. I think it's funny. If you want to answer it in our issue of the Tatler this month, send me word what to say, and I'll see to it. Hurry up and get well. We all miss you lots, especially in Latin class. Love to the rest.

"Ange."

Betty opened the paper at the tenth page and read:

IMPORTANT NEWS ITEM.

"Sudden disappearance of valuable mump germs. Last seen in a silver trophy cup on or about February twenty-fifth. Seddon Hall basket ball team under suspicion of theft, but no arrests have been made. Any information regarding same will be gratefully received."

"That settles it." Betty stopped reading to laugh. "We took their mump germs with a vengeance.

"Means they've got it, too," laughed Lois.

"Of course we'll have to answer it," Polly said.

The next few days the composition of a fitting reply occupied all their time. They wrote and discarded a dozen answers before finally deciding on a poem of Betty's. The Tatler went to press with instructions to print it on the first page, and the Whitehead girls, when they got their copy, laughed long and heartily, for this is what they read:

"Eight little germs lurked in a cup
  All on a pleasant day.
Eight little maids they spied that cup
  When they went out to play.
They thought they'd take it home with them;
  They didn't know, you see,
The mumpy germs were waiting there
  As slyly as could be.
But when they took the cup, alas!
  Those eight germs gave eight jumps
And landed in those eight maids' throats,
  And gave them each the mumps."

CHAPTER XVII

SPRING

The months of March and April had come and gone. The days had passed in unvarying monotony for the most part.

Now and again, however, some little incident found its place and added the necessary interest to the school life. The long term after Christmas is always tiring, and Easter vacation had come as a relief. By the time this chapter opens the grounds of Seddon Hall gave proof of spring — warm days and sunshine beckoned the girls out of doors, and early flowers rewarded their frequent rambles in the woods. In less than three weeks school would close, and another Senior class would graduate. Polly and Lois had seen the same thing happen year after year, but now that the time was approaching for them to go, they experienced the same feeling of regret and wonder that every girl knows who has ever finished and received a diploma.

Fortunately they did not have much time to wonder at the coming change in their lives, for there are many events that crowd themselves into the last few weeks of a Senior's school life, occupying most of her time.

To-day was a particularly busy one. There was a Senior class meeting to decide on the Senior play. The photographer was coming to take the class picture. There was a basket ball practice, for Field Day was not far off, and an art exhibition in the evening. The latter was an entirely new idea instigated by Miss Crosby. Every girl who could draw or paint had offered the best her portfolio could yield, and these had been framed and hung on the walls of the Assembly Hall.

A committee of judges composed of the faculty and two important friends of Miss Crosby, who had promised to come up especially, were to award a medal for the best painting and for the best sketch. Add to all of this, the fact that Louise Preston and Florence Guile — two of the old girls — were expected on a visit, and you have an idea of the events to which the Seniors looked forward, as they jumped out of bed at the first sound of the rising bell.

And Polly and Lois had another cause for excitement. To-day was the day of the inter-collegiate track meet, and Bob was running in one of the relay races. So many school duties had made it impossible for them to go, but Jim had promised to wire them the results.

Betty met Polly and Lois, as usual, in Roman Alley, and they discussed the plans for the day, as the water ran in their tubs.

"Do you think the Dorothys are going to vote against 'The Merchant of Venice'?" Betty asked, dropping down on the lower step of the stairs. "I'll simply refuse to act, if we have to have Tennyson's 'Princess.' I think it's a silly thing."

"Oh, Bet!" Lois protested.

"Well, I do, and we'd never learn all those yards of verse by Commencement."

"I think we can make the Dorothys agree," Polly said, confidently. "Mrs. Baird is coming to the meeting, and I know she'd rather we gave the 'Merchant of Venice.'"

"What about the class picture?" Lois asked. "How are we going to have it taken — all standing in a stiff group, as usual?"

"Jemima, no!" Betty exclaimed. "The officers all sit, I insist; else what proof have we of our importance?"

"Bet, do be sensible," Polly pleaded. "This is really important. Oh, here comes Ange," she said as a kimono came in sight around the bend in the stairs.

"Come on, lazy one; we're having a meeting," Betty called. "Subject under discussion, the Senior class picture. Have you any valuable suggestions to offer!"

"Yes, I have," Angela replied, unexpectedly, "and it's a very clever one, if I do say it myself," she drawled. "I may as well warn you that if you don't agree with me, I'll be awfully offended."

"Then maybe you'd better not tell us," teased Lois.

"Oh, but I will. Now listen to me." Angela sat down beside Polly. "It's about the picture. Of course you all want something different, don't you? You know our class has always been noted — "

"For its originality," Betty finished for her.

"Yes, we know, go on," encouraged Polly.

"Well, I thought that instead of an everyday white dress and diploma kind of a pose, we'd have a very informal, sailor suit, you know, group taken.

"Good idea! It would be much simpler and better taste," Lois agreed.

"Now wait," Angela went on. "I haven't finished. Instead of having it taken indoors, with a plain wall for a background, it would be much nicer to have it taken out of doors, either on the Senior porch or out on one of the rocks, side of the pond."

"That would be perfect," Polly exclaimed, enthusiastically.

"No class has ever done it before, and I know Mrs. Baird will be overjoyed at the idea of having something a little different from those awful set pictures her office is lined with."

"It is a good scheme," Betty said slowly. "But oh, my children! Do you think for one moment that the Dorothys will ever agree?"

"You leave the Dorothys to me," Polly said. "I'll see that they agree to everything."

The meeting was held immediately after school in one of the classrooms. Mrs. Baird was there, and sat beside Lois. Everything was very formal and quite according to Parliamentary rules.

Lois mentioned the subjects that were to be discussed, and before any one else had a chance to speak, Polly rose and asked to be permitted to offer a suggestion.

When it had been granted, she laid before them Angela's idea for the picture. Mrs. Baird was so charmed that she forgot to be formal, in her enthusiastic praise of it.

When that point was settled, Lois mentioned the play.

Betty jumped up at the first words and gave several very good reasons in favor of the "Merchant of Venice." Evelin and Helen agreed with her and though the two Dorothys voted for "The Princess," the majority was in Betty's favor.

It was decided that Mrs. Baird and Miss Porter should cast each girl in her part.

Towards the end of the meeting, there was a knock on the door. Polly opened it. Louise Preston and Florence Guile stood in the hall.

"Don't let us disturb anything," Louise said, "but Miss Hale told us Mrs. Baird was here."

Polly pulled them into the room. "Oh, but I'm glad to see you," she cried. "We thought you'd never get here."

The meeting broke up at once, for the girls crowded round to welcome them. They had both been Seniors when the present class were Freshmen. Now they were Juniors at College, but like most of the Seddon Hall graduates, they always came back, at least once a year. The girls were all delighted to see them for they had been two of the most popular girls who had ever been in the school.

When the greetings were over, Polly and Lois claimed them, and carried them off to the gym. Louise had been Captain in her Senior year and was now on her college team, and Polly wanted her advice.

"Now, Lou, tell me just exactly what you think," she said after the game was over, and they were all four in her room.

"I think your team is fine, Polly, really," Louise said, sincerely, "but—"

"Yes, it's that but, I want to hear about," Polly prompted.

"The guards are your weak point. That one girl made four fouls. Miss Stewart didn't see them all, but I did," Louise said.

"That's Eleanor Trent, she's used to boys' rules," Lois explained.

"Then she's hopeless," Florence said with finality, "and she'll never get over it."

"Who's the girl that was guarding you?" Louise asked.

"That's Maud Banks; she's been a sub for only a little while," Polly said. "I put her on to take the place of a girl who didn't come back after Easter. Why?"

"I think she ought to be on the big team," Louise declared. "She's a splendid player."

Polly considered. "I guess you're right," she said.

"You and Lo and Bet pass as well as ever," Florence said. "Lois, where did you get that Princeton banner?" she asked, changing the subject abruptly.

"Frank gave it to me."

"It's coming down to-night and my banner takes its place," Polly said; "that is, if something happens."

"What?" Louise demanded.

But Polly's explanation was cut short by a timid tap at the door.

"Come in," called Lois. It was Phylis and Janet.

"We've come to take you out for a walk, sister," Phylis said to Florence. "You promised you'd come back right after practice and you didn't."

Florence laughed. "Mercy, what a rude awakening. Here I've been feeling just as if I were back again and then my small sister knocks at the door and reminds me I'm only a visitor!"

"Their coming makes me think of the way you two used to knock at our door," Louise said. "Remember?"

"Only Lo and Poll were never as respectful as Jane and Phylis," Florence teased, putting her arm around her sister. "They used to bounce in unannounced and eat up all our peanut butter."

"Florence, you shouldn't talk like that," her sister admonished her. "You forget Polly and Lois are Seniors," she said with dignity.

"A thousand pardons!" Florence laughed. "So they are."

"I see you have your defenders just as we had," Louise remarked.

"I think it's time to go," Janet announced, and she didn't understand why everybody laughed.

"Tell us about the exhibition to-night," Louise said, as they started for their walk, and Janet explained:

"All the girls who are at all good, put things in," she concluded. "These two friends of Miss Crosby are both artists and they're very important. I hope Lois gets the prize."

"Do you think she will?" Florence asked.

"I don't know, but Maud Banks says she's sure to," Janet replied.

Polly and Lois, after their visitors had left, hurried back into their sailor suits and joined the rest of the Seniors in the reception room, where the photographer was waiting.

Lois explained about the picture and led the way to the pond. He selected a rock and grouped the girls around it. This took so much time, that Lois hurried to the studio to find it was too late to make the one or two alterations on her canvas that she had wanted to.

"Oh, dear," she said to Miss Crosby; "I never realized how late it was getting. What will I do?"

"You'll leave your canvas just as it is," Miss Crosby answered. "I'm glad the light is poor. I didn't want you to make any changes. Come down to Assembly Hall and help me to hang up the rest of the sketches, will you?" she asked.

The two artists who were to act as judges came in time for dinner. The girls had a glimpse of them as they passed the guests' dining-room.

"Why, they're men," Betty exclaimed. "One's fat, old and bald, and the other one's young. I thought they were going to be women."

"No, of course not." Lois laughed. "Miss Crosby told me all about them, they're quite famous. Do you know I'm scared to death," she admitted.

There was no set time for the exhibition that night. The Assembly Hall was open at seven-thirty, and the girls came in and looked at the pictures when they wanted to.

The two imposing visitors, who both wore tortoise shell rimmed glasses on broad black ribbons, walked about glancing at a picture now and then, and talking to the faculty.

"They make me awfully nervous; let's get out. I think some of the girls are dancing in English Room," Lois said. She was with Polly and Louise and Florence.

"Then how will we know who gets the medal?" Louise inquired.

"The bell's going to ring at nine o'clock," Polly explained. "Then everybody will come back, and the winner's names will be announced from the platform.

"Well, let's look once more at Lois' canvas," Florence said. "I'm crazy about it."

They crossed the room and stopped before a picture of an apple orchard in Springtime. Lois had chosen to paint it, because it was her favorite spot in the grounds, and she had put into it all the joy and sunshine of a May-day.

"Lo, it's good," Polly whispered earnestly. "It makes me want to dance."

"Have you seen Maud's sketches, they're great," Lois said. The critics were standing near and she felt suddenly self-conscious.

"I think the one of the chicken yard is awfully clever, but, of course I love the yellow dog best of all."

Maud, when she had heard of the exhibit, had chosen her puppy friend for one of her models. The girls admired the clever result, and then left the room.

At nine o'clock the bell rang. It was five minutes before all the girls were back in the room, and Lois was among the last. She was almost afraid to listen for the names. When everything was quiet, the older of the two men came to the edge of the platform — the medals in his hand.

"This unexpected, but none the less, charming evening," he began; "has caused me a great deal of pleasure. It is a privilege to be among you."

"Oh, do hurry," groaned Polly.

"And I am indebted to our friend Miss Crosby, for the honor. With the assistance of your faculty—whose judgment I am sure you respect most heartily," he added, with a quiet smile; "I have chosen that very delightful painting of the apple orchard—without hesitation—as the most noteworthy and promising canvas in the room. It is with the greatest pleasure that I present Miss Lois Farwell with the medal."

Lois walked up to the platform. Her head was swimming and all the color had left her cheeks.

"Thank you," she said, as the medal on its purple ribbon slipped into her hand. She seemed to be treading on air as she walked back to Polly.

Maud received the other medal for her clever and original treatment of the yellow dog; her comment was typical.

"Oh, I say, thanks a lot!" she said, as she accepted it.

Miss Crosby detained Lois after the girls had all gone and introduced her to the two men. She heard their praise and criticism of her work with a beating heart. She was tempted to think it was all a dream, when she was back in her room, but the card she held in her hand, that the artist had given her, was proof of reality.

"Polly," she said, excitedly, "you should have heard the nice things he said to me, and he told me that if I wanted advice, to come to him. Imagine! I'm much too thrilled to go tamely to bed."

"I know," Polly agreed; "my heart was in my throat when he was talking. I thought he'd never stop. To-morrow I'm going to write Aunt Kate all about it. Think how delighted she'll be."

Lois smiled happily. "I know she will. She's always been so adorably interested in everything. I wish I had something to eat," she finished prosaically.

"I'll go see if Bet and Ange have anything," Polly offered.

She tip-toed out of the door — for the good night bell had rung — and started toward Betty's room. One of the housemaids was just coming down the corridor.

"Here's a telegram for you, Miss Polly," she said. "Mrs. Baird told me to bring it up; it's just come."

Polly took the yellow envelope and tore it open. "Lois," she cried, joyfully, rushing back to their room. "Look! a wire."

"Bob a hero — he's won his letter."

(Signed) "Jim."

"Isn't that wonderful?" Polly demanded. "Now we'll never get to sleep," she added, laughing.

CHAPTER XVIII

FIELD DAY

The two weeks after the exhibition had been taken up by final examinations — an anxious time for the graduating class.

Seddon Hall kept up a high standard and no girl could receive a diploma unless her marks showed a high average. When the papers were all corrected, a notice was posted on the bulletin board of the girls who had failed. Betty called it the black list.

"I know perfectly well my name will lead them all," she said. They were waiting in the corridor, for the list was to be posted to-day. "And if the Spartan has anything to do with it, she'll probably print it extra large," she added.

Angela and Polly and Lois were with her, and to a less extent they shared her fears.

"It really doesn't matter so much to you," Angela said; "You're none of you going to college, but imagine if I flunk anything."

"You can make it up this summer," Lois said.

"Yes, and take entrance exams. No, thanks; I'd prefer entering on certificate," Angela drawled.

Evelin and Helen came out of the study hall. "Any news yet?" Evelin asked.

Betty shook her head. "No," she said, solemnly, "it must be a very long list they are making out. What are you two nervous about?"

"Everything in general," Helen said, hopelessly, "but history in particular."

"The Dorothys are calmly indifferent," Polly remarked. "Why aren't they here?"

"They're coming now," Evelin said. "No news?" she called.

Dot Mead stopped half way down the corridor.

"This suspense is killing me," she said, "we've been trying to study our parts, but it's no use."

"This awful delay argues the very worst," Betty said. "We've all flunked everything, and all those beautiful new diplomas will never be used. What a cruel waste."

"Betty, do try and be a little more cheerful," Polly pleaded; "can't you see my knees are knocking together? Oh, if I ever live through this week!"

"That's the way I feel," Lois agreed, forlornly. "I've a million and one things to do and no time. Think of it, Field Day to-morrow!"

"And that means, we ought to be practicing all day to-day," Evelin said.

"Exactly, but if I practice to-day, I won't know my part for the play. I do wish Portia hadn't talked so much," Lois answered.

"Then there's all the things to see to about the dance," Angela added.

"And the Commencement Hymn to learn," Helen reminded them.

"The game's the most important," Polly said, decidedly, "but I don't want any of the team to do any practicing. Some one would be sure to get hurt."

"What are you going to do about Eleanor?" Betty asked.

"Give her a chance," Polly told her; "but she knows that the first foul she makes I take her out and put Maud in."

"Good! was she hurt?" Lois asked.

"No; she understands, and she's promised to be very careful—"

"Oh, where—oh, where is that list?" Dorothy Lansing returned to the subject with a sigh.

They waited in silence for a while longer, and at last their patience was rewarded. They heard a step on the stair and Mrs. Baird came towards them.

"What is this? a Senior class meeting?" she asked, smiling.

"No," Betty answered for them all. "We're waiting in agonized suspense for the exam list."

"Why, you poor children," Mrs. Baird laughed; "there isn't any list this year. You all passed in everything."

139

There was an exclamation of joyful relief from the girls.

"Thank goodness!" from Polly. "Now we can breathe in peace. Oh, but I'm glad!"

"Wasn't it fortunate I happened to come up," Mrs. Baird laughed. "You might have waited all afternoon. I really came to tell you that I have made arrangements at the hotel for all your families for the night before Commencement, and to find out if you expected any one here for the game to-morrow. Your mother and father are coming, Betty. I heard from them to-day."

"My uncle is coming if he possibly can," Polly added.

"Mother and Dad will surely be here," Lois said, "and so will Bob; but he'll be late."

"There will be more visitors than usual for to-morrow, won't there?" Mrs. Baird asked. "You'll have to win the game, Polly."

"If I don't, I'll hide somewhere and never show my face again," Polly answered. "Think how awful it would be to lose on our own floor, and with visitors to witness the defeat."

"Well, don't worry about it," Mrs. Baird advised. "You know the best team always wins."

"We beat last year. So this year it's their turn," Angela teased.

The next day the visitors began to arrive on the noon train. All morning the girls had been busy decorating the gym and practicing songs. By luncheon time everything was ready, and the Fenwick school team arrived in one big carryall, followed by another, filled with their friends and well-wishers. Polly, as captain, was so busy with her duties that she had only a minute now and then to think of the game.

Dr. and Mrs. Farwell came among the first guests and she and Lois happened to be in the front hall when they arrived.

"Where's Uncle Roddy?" Polly asked, after she had greeted them, "and where, oh, where is Bob?"

"Roddy will be up later," the doctor told her.

"And Bob may not be able to come," Mrs. Farwell explained. "You see he wants to be here surely for the dance — "

"Jim's coming too, isn't he?" Lois interrupted. "He wrote he would."

"Yes; they'll both be here to-morrow without fail," her mother assured her. "And Bob will come to-day, if he possibly can."

But there was no sign of him when Polly glanced up at the visitors' gallery, as the Seddon Hall team marched into the gym at two o'clock.

"There's a train due now; maybe he's on that," Lois whispered under cover of the singing.

"What a bunch of people," Betty exclaimed, looking around the room.

Every seat in the gallery was filled with friends and relatives, and the girls had been forced to find places on the floor downstairs.

The teams stopped and faced each other in the center of the floor. Polly's heart sank; somehow the Fenwick team looked more imposing in gym suits than she had expected, and she remembered that one of the guards had told her they had won every game they had played that year.

"Perhaps," she thought, "it's just as well Bob isn't here."

They took their places on the floor, and Miss Stewart blew the whistle. In a game that really counts, there is no sound so exciting as that first whistle. It means so much. Betty rose to her toes at the sound of it, and faced the opposing jumping center.

"I think I'd like the first ball," the Fenwick girl said, laughing.

"Sorry, but you can't have it," Betty replied, bounding into the air; "it's mine!" She batted it back towards Fanny.

"Good!" Polly whispered to Lois, and raised her left hand above her head.

But the Fenwick side center intercepted Fanny's pass and, before they knew it, the ball was down at the other end. Evelin failed to guard her forward and, after a high toss, the ball fell into the basket.

Dorothy Mead, as official score keeper, drew a 2 slowly on the blackboard. Fanny felt the fault was entirely hers and turned appealing eyes to her captain.

"Cheer up!" Polly called. "That's only one; dodge her next time."

But Fanny didn't get a chance to even touch the ball, for Betty lost the toss up, and the ball was spirited away to the other goal. Evelin fought hard, but Eleanor was so busy thinking about the lines that the Fenwick team made another basket.

"Oh, this is awful! I never saw Eleanor so slow," Lois said.

Betty lost the next toss up, too, but, fortunately, Evelin stopped it and threw to Fanny. She passed to Betty, and Lois waited for it near the line, but her guard kept her from getting it. They fought hard in the center for the next few minutes. Eleanor got so excited that she stepped over the line, the whistle blew, and the Fenwick forward made a basket. The score was five to nothing.

Eleanor looked at Polly, but she shook her head.

"The first half is almost up," she said to Lois. "I don't want to change yet."

Fanny fumbled the next ball Betty sent her.

"That's inexcusable," Lois declared, angrily, and Betty stamped her foot in rage. Fanny began to cry.

"That's the end," Lois said; "you can't put a sub in for her."

"No; but I can do something equally as good," Polly replied, quietly. "Wait till this half is over." It was like her to be carelessly hopeful, when everybody else was in despair.

The Fenwick team scored again before the longed-for whistle blew.

"There's Bob and Uncle Roddy," Polly said, just as the ball dropped into the basket. "He's looking at the score," she added, laughing.

Lois stared at her in amazement.

"Poll, what's the matter with you?" she demanded. "Do you realize that the score is seven to nothing!"

"Yes," Polly replied in unruffled tones, "but there's another half, and you seem to have forgotten that."

The school broke into a song and the teams sat down for a much needed rest. Polly looked up at the gallery and nodded merrily to Bob. Then she went up to Eleanor.

"I'm sorry; but I'm going to put Maud in the next half," she said.

"Oh, thank goodness!" Eleanor exclaimed. "I've lost my nerve."

"Get ready, Maud," Polly said, going over to the subs; "you've got a hard job ahead."

"Righto!" Maud said, instantly; and Polly walked over to Fanny. She was crying on Betty's shoulder.

"Take me out," she sobbed, as Polly came up. "I'm no good on earth."

"You are quite right; you aren't," Polly replied, sternly. "I never saw such a silly exhibition of flunk. If I had any one to put in your place, I would; but you know I haven't."

Betty looked up in surprise. She thought Polly was being a little too hard on poor Fanny.

"I never saw such poor plays in my life," Polly continued, relentlessly. "You seemed to enjoy flunking. If you'd stop thinking of Jack and John and the rest of your admirers and pay a little attention to the game, we might stand a chance," she concluded, coldly.

"Why, Polly!" Fanny dried her eyes. "You shouldn't talk to me like that. I did the best I could, and I wasn't thinking of boys," she denied, angrily, "and you know it."

Polly refused to even listen. She turned her back on Fanny and sat down beside Lois.

"And that's all right," she said contentedly.

"What is?" Lois demanded. "Poll, we haven't a chance."

"Oh, yes, we have; just watch."

The whistle blew for the second half and the teams returned to their places. Instead of tears, Fanny's eyes flashed indignant protest, and her mouth was set in a firm line.

Maud took Eleanor's place, much to the latter's satisfaction. Betty won the first toss up, passed the ball to Fanny. She bounced it to line and threw it to Polly. She was so angry that she literally fired the ball. Polly caught it, tossed it to Lois, and she made a clean basket.

"What did I tell you?" she said; "we're going to win this game."

They played hard for the rest of the half. Maud persistently refused to let the Fenwick forward even touch the ball. In her attempt to get beyond the reach of Maud's guarding arm, she went over the line, and Polly made a basket on the foul.

The spectators were breathless as the score mounted up—7-3, 7-5 and at last 7-7. The girls cheered encouragement and Bob and Uncle Roddy clapped so hard that Polly and Lois looked up and waved.

Lois had just caught a ball that Betty threw and was aiming for a basket when the whistle blew.

"Now, what!" Betty demanded. "We can't stop with a tie."

Miss Stewart consulted the two captains.

"We will play an extra two minutes," she said, "to decide. Ready!"

It was a tense second. The school groaned as the Fenwick center won the toss, but they had forgotten Maud. She jumped high in the air and batted the ball back to Betty, who passed it to Fanny, and then ran to the line to receive it again. Lois was waiting for it and passed it low to Polly and dashed to the goal post. Polly threw it back to her and she threw for the basket. There was an agonized silence as the ball tottered on the iron rim, that broke into a shout of triumph as it dropped in the basket, a fraction of a minute before the whistle blew.

Seddon Hall had won—a splendid victory—and Polly's dream was realized. The girls crowded around her and cheered; then lifted her according to custom, shoulder high, and carried her around the room.

"Where's Fanny Gerard?" she asked as soon as they put her down before the cup she had won.

"Here!" Betty called, pulling the reluctant center to her.

Polly threw her arms around her. "Fanny, will you ever forgive me?" she said. "I didn't mean a word of all those horrid things I said — not one. I only did it to make you mad. I knew if you could only begin to rage, you'd get back your nerve, and you did; you played like a little fury — but oh, how I hated to do it!"

Fanny threw back her head and laughed with relief. "Oh, Polly!" she exclaimed, "I thought you really meant it."

Maud accepted Polly's praise with genuine pleasure. For once her stolid indifference gave way to natural enthusiasm. Mrs. Baird presented Polly with the cup, and the Fenwick captain added to her joy by telling her that she had never seen such a wonderful exhibition of generalship. Dr. and Mrs. Farwell, with Uncle Roddy and Bob were waiting at the door as the girls came out bundled up in their sweaters.

"Good for you, Polly!" Bob said, enthusiastically. "That certainly was a ripping game, and you deserve a whole lot of credit. I take back everything I ever said about your girls' basket ball. Let's see the cup," he added.

Polly showed it to him.

"I'm proud of you, Tiddledewinks," Uncle Roddy said, "and Lois, too. You have a splendid eye. That last goal was well made." He put his hand on her shoulder.

"I'm dumbfounded!" the doctor exclaimed. "I had no idea girls did anything as strenuous as this."

"You must be tired out?" Mrs. Farwell said, "and you'll catch cold. Do hurry back to school and change."

Polly and Lois started.

"I wish Jim had been here," Lois called over her shoulder to Bob. "Perhaps he might have changed his mind about basket ball being a good enough girls' game," she said.

"He'll be here to-morrow," Bob replied. "And you can trust me to see that his mind is changed," he promised.

CHAPTER XIX
THE SENIOR DANCE

History classroom, converted temporarily into a dressing room, was a scene of busy confusion. The Seniors were being "made up" — a woman had come from New York especially for the purpose.

It was almost time for the play to begin and everybody was in a hurry. Outside the Assembly Hall was rapidly filling and the murmur of voices penetrated to the dressing room.

"There must be a perfect swarm of visitors," Betty said. "I know the minute I get on that stage I'll forget every one of my lines," she added, as she looked critically at herself in the glass. She was playing the part of Shylock, and her long beard and gray wig disguised her almost beyond recognition.

"Do you think I need some more lines on my face?" she asked Miss Crosby, who was acting as stage manager.

"No, Betty dear, I don't; I think you're quite ugly enough," Miss Crosby answered her. "Are you ready, Polly?"

"No; I'm still struggling with this sash," Polly answered, coming out from behind a screen dressed as Bassanio.

"I'll fix it. There!" Miss Crosby tied the refractory sash and then stood off to view the effect. "You make a very gallant and graceful Bassanio," she said.

"Where's my Portia?" Polly inquired.

Lois was being "made up"; so she could only laugh in response. She was charming in a full black velvet gown, trimmed with heavy white lace, and her hair was crowned by a cap of pearls.

Angela, in dark green, was no less lovely as Nerissa. Evelin made a dignified Antonio, and Dot Mead a jaunty Gratiano. Helen played the double role of Salarino and the Moor, while Dorothy Lansing took The Prince of Arragon and the Gaoler.

On account of the small number of Seniors, all of the lesser characters had been omitted, and the play had been cut down to three acts.

The first — the Venetian street scene, where Antonio bargains with Shylock. The second — the choosing of the caskets, and the third — the courtroom.

Angela, who was industriously shaking powder into her new satin slipper because it hurt, began reciting her lines:

"'Your Father was ever virtuous; and holy men at their death have good inspirations—'"

"Do keep still, Ange," Betty begged; "you'll get me all mixed up. 'Oh, upright judge — a Daniel — come prepare—'" she murmured to herself.

Lois in the other corner of the room was chanting: "'The quality of mercy is not strained — it droppeth like the gentle dew from Heaven upon the place beneath. It is thrice blest—' There, I know I'll get that wrong," she broke off — "it's 'twice blest,' and I always say 'thrice.'"

"You're far too generous with your blessings," Polly laughed. "I feel perfectly sure that I will giggle right out when you say: 'You see me Lord Bassanio as I am—' you know."

"Don't you dare look at me," Lois warned, "or I'll laugh, too. Mercy, listen to those people! I'm going to peep." She opened the door a crack and looked out into the Assembly Hall. She saw Maud and Fanny, who were acting as two of the ushers, seating the new arrivals.

"The hall's jammed," she told the girls. "How many guests have you to-night, Dot?" she asked.

"Six! My mother, two girl cousins of mine and three boys."

"I expect five," Evelin said. "I hope they're all here. Did you notice two lanky men, a girl that looks like me, and my mother and father?"

"No, I didn't," Lois said; "that is, I can't recognize them from your description."

"Wasn't it a shame your mother couldn't come, Betty?" Polly said. "But, of course, Dick is here," she teased.

"No, he's not," Lois laughed. "I'd have seen his red head in the crowd if he had been."

"He's coming with John Frisby and Ange's sister and brother-in-law," Betty said, without paying any attention to Lois' teasing.

"There'll be at least twenty couples for the dance," Polly said. "That means the room won't look half empty, the way it did last year."

"I hope there's enough sherbet," Evelin said; "boys always eat twice as much as you expect them to."

"Well, there are cakes enough to feed a whole army," Dorothy Lansing added. "I know, for I ordered them."

"The orchestra is here. Oh, bother that buckle! it's sure to come off," Helen exclaimed.

"Has the sherbet come, does anybody know?" Angela asked.

"They promised it by six o'clock," Dot Mead replied; "it's surely here by now."

"It's time for the curtain," Miss Crosby called, as she came down from the stage, where she had been putting the last finishing touches to the Venetian street. "Are you ready?"

Polly and Angela and Helen jumped up.

"Don't forget your cue, Betty," Angela warned, "and don't you dare make me laugh."

Miss Crosby gave the signal for the lights to be turned off and a low murmur of anticipation ran through the Assembly Hall as the curtain rose.

Betty's clever interpretation of Shylock won the applause for the first act.

"Jemima! I'm glad that's over," she said as the curtain rang down. "The grease paint is all running down my cheeks. It's awfully hot up there."

They heard the audience still applauding.

"Go take a curtain call, Betty," Miss Crosby called. "All of you, hurry up! Lois, are you and Angela ready for the next act?"

It is hard to say who held the stage during the casket scene. Angela was sweet as Nerissa, and Polly made such a charming lover that she was especially applauded. Lois delighted every one as Portia, but, of course, her real triumph came in the next act.

It is one of the hardest things in the world to recite lines with which your audience is familiar and put sufficient new meaning in them to hold their attention. It is so easy to fall into a sing-song chant, particularly with a long speech. But Lois did it. She gave each word its proper stress and the soft mellow quality of her voice gained her extra praise.

It was a tired, but happily contented cast that took the encore after the final curtain, and the audience were enthusiastic in their applause.

"And now, for the dance," Polly exclaimed, as they hurried back to the dressing room to change their costumes. "I wish we could go as we are —"

"Why, Polly, you shock me," Betty laughed. "I can't imagine eating sherbet with this beard."

"They are pushing back the chairs; hear them?" Lois said. "Do hurry, Poll."

They finished dressing, and joined their party waiting for them in one corner of the room. Jim Thorp and Bob were extravagant in their congratulations.

"I expect that Lo will be starring in less than a year. How many people have called you a born actress, little sister?" he asked.

"Oh, at least a million!" Lois replied; for she was not to be teased.

"How do you like being a man, Polly?" Jim inquired. "You were so dashing and debonair, that I bet every fellow in the room felt big and clumsy in comparison."

"That pretty girl who played Nerissa was fine. I'd like to meet her," Bob said, "and you must introduce Jim to Betty; I want him to see her without the beard."

"All right; come on, and let's find them; they'll be together," Polly suggested as the music started.

"Oh, let's have one dance first!" Bob said.

After the dance ended, all the girls tried to introduce their friends to one another. It was a little confusing, for all the boys wanted to dance with every girl. Polly was so busy, meeting and dancing with different partners, that she didn't see Bob again until much later in the evening. He was standing in one corner of the room and he looked very warm.

"Let's go out," he suggested. "It's so awfully hot in here; it's not against the rules, or anything, is it?" he added, as Polly hesitated.

She laughed. "No, of course not; but I was trying to remember who I had the next dance with," she said.

"With me," Bob assured her promptly. "Come on; I have your scarf in my pocket." They slipped out of one of the long windows at the end of the hall and walked toward the pond.

"Bob, do you realize that this is my last night at Seddon Hall?" Polly said, seriously. Bob nodded. "Yes, to-morrow you get your nice, beribboned diploma, or, I suppose it's beribboned; is it?"

"Yes!" Polly answered absently.

"Lucky you."

"Why?"

"To have finished. There's nothing more thoroughly satisfactory than finishing something," Bob said, earnestly.

"But some things are too wonderful ever to finish," Polly objected, looking down at the stars reflected in the pond. "I'm simply broken-hearted at the thought of leaving to-morrow. It's all been so fine. Why, Bobby, what will life away from Seddon Hall be like?"

"Whatever you make it, I suppose," Bob said, wisely. Polly was silent for a time.

"Well," she said at last, "whatever I do, or whatever happens to me, it will never be quite as nice as Seddon Hall."

"What a happy outlook," Bob teased. "Polly, you're indulging in the blues. Stop it!" he commanded.

Polly laughed and gave herself a little shake. "All right! It's the stars, they always make me sad; come on, let's go back and dance."

As they returned they met Betty and Dick. They were hurrying around the corner of the house.

"Whither away?" Polly called, gaily.

"Oh, Poll, the most awful thing has happened!" Betty explained, when they came up to them. "The sherbet didn't come and all the class are tearing their hair; we're out looking for it."

"Better join the expedition," Dick laughed.

"Betty tells me there are no less than seven back doors to this place, and the sherbet may be melting at any one of them."

"Oh, Dick, it's serious!" Betty said, crossly. "Dot Mead called up the caterer and he said it had been delivered," she explained to Polly.

"A tragedy!" Bob exclaimed. "I must have sherbet; the party will be ruined without it."

"Of course it will," Betty answered; "you can't do just with chicken salad. It's got to be found. You go that way and we'll go this. Look at every door, and perhaps we'll find it."

They started in opposite directions, but when they met outside of the Assembly Hall a few minutes later the sherbet was still missing.

"I'm going to tell Mrs. Baird," Betty said; "maybe she can suggest something to do. Dick, you wait here with Polly and Bob. I'll be right back."

And she disappeared through the window.

"Do you suppose," Polly said, suddenly—"I have an idea. Come with me, both of you." She ran down the road, regardless of satin slippers, as far as the gym. "They may have left it here by mistake," she said to the boys.

Bob ran to the door. "Here it is!" he exclaimed. He pointed to the six buckets packed full of ice.

"What will we do with it?" Dick inquired. "Carry it back to Betty?"

"No; we'll unpack it here—ugh! The ice is all slushy." She stood back to save her dress.

"We'll do it," Bob said. "You look out. Here Dick, dump them."

"You'll ruin your clothes," Polly protested. "Wait and I'll get some one from the house."

"Never!" Dick declared, "wait even an instant while this precious stuff melts; I should say not."

"All right, you unpack it; be careful of the tins, the covers fall off sometimes, and the salt gets in the ice cream," she warned. "I'll go find Betty."

She found her on the Senior porch. She was just coming out with one of the maids.

"We've found it!" Polly called to her.

"Jemima! where?" Betty demanded.

"At the gym. The driver must have just dumped it down at the first door he came to. The boys are unpacking it."

Fifteen minutes later the sherbet, a little melted and, perhaps a trifle salty, was served in glass cups and no one but the agonized Seniors and Dick and Bob knew of the narrow escape.

The rescuing party joined Lois and Jim over in one corner of the room.

"It's delicious," Bob said, feelingly. "Jim, did you ever unpack ice cream cans that were completely surrounded by slush?" he asked, casually.

"No!" Jim said, wonderingly. "Why?"

"Didn't you? You should have."

"Do it the next warm night when you're all dressed up."

"It's a great way to cool off," Dick advised.

"What are they talking about, Poll?" Lois demanded.

Polly explained. "It was such a lark watching them!" she concluded, laughing.

"I'm going to write," Betty began, and then stopped abruptly.

"Write what?" Dick asked.

Betty's expression changed. "Jemima!" she said slowly; "I was going to say, that the next composition I wrote would be on the Quest of the Missing Sherbet and then I suddenly remembered that I wouldn't have to write any more. This is our last night," she added, solemnly.

Polly and Lois looked at her. The smiles faded from their lips, and they ate the rest of the sherbet in silence.

CHAPTER XX
COMMENCEMENT

Commencement was over. The service in the little church had been very simple, but very beautiful. The Seniors dressed in the daintiest of white lawn dresses had received their diplomas, and marched slowly down the center aisle.

There had been a hurried scramble back to school. A change of clothes and then the long line of carriages had started for the station.

Polly stood on the last step of the Senior porch. Lois and her mother and father had just left for the train. They were returning to Albany for a little while before leaving for the summer vacation.

Polly was going back to New York with Uncle Roddy in his car. She watched the last carriage out of sight. There was an unnatural silence about the school buildings and she looked dejectedly at the deserted grounds. Uncle Roddy was saying good-by to Mrs. Baird at the door.

"Are you ready to start, Tiddledewinks?" he asked, handing her suitcase to the chauffeur, and waiting to help her in the car.

Polly turned to Mrs. Baird.

"I suppose so; it's all over and I can't think of any excuse to stay," she said, making a pitiful attempt at a smile.

"Dear child," Mrs. Baird said, affectionately, "don't talk like that. Seddon Hall always has a place for all her girls; a diploma doesn't make any difference and I can promise that there will always be an extra warm welcome for a certain little girl."

Polly kissed her impulsively. "I'll be back so often next year that you'll get tired of me," she laughed, as she got into the car. Mrs. Baird waved until they turned the bend in the road. Polly looked back in a last farewell, until the buildings on the hill were a tiny speck. Then she turned to her uncle.

"Uncle Roddy," she said, seriously, "do you remember what you said to me the first night I was home, after my Freshman year?"

"No, dear; not particularly," Uncle Roddy replied. "What was it?"

"You told me that you hoped every year of my life would be happier than the last," she told him. "Well it has, up until now, but I feel suddenly lost. What am I going to do?"

Uncle Roddy laughed and he took her hand.

"You're going to begin a new chapter in life, dear," he said, seriously, "and I think you'll find it more interesting and fuller than the last."

"Will I?" Polly asked, wonderingly.

"Yes," Uncle Roddy said, confidently. "It will be fuller and more worth while. I know I can trust my Tiddledewinks to make it that."

Polly pondered in silence for a few minutes. Then her frown disappeared and she gave herself a little shake thereby dismissing all regrets. She turned to look back in the direction of the school.

"Good-by, dear old Seddon Hall," she said, smiling, "I'm ready for the next chapter."

THE END